Question: How do you find the perfect man?

Answer: Read on....

Texas Grooms Wanted! is a brand-new miniseries in Harlequin Romance®.

Meet three wonderful heroines who are all looking for very special Texas men—their future husbands!

Good men may be hard to find, but these women have experts on hand. They've all signed up with the Yellow Rose Matchmakers. The oldest—and the best!—matchmaking service in San Antonio, Texas, the Yellow Rose guarantees to find any woman her perfect partner....

So, for the cutest cowboys in the whole state of Texas, read:

Only cowboys need apply....

Name: Day Leclaire

Age: Old enough to have a fourteen-year-old son. (Of course, precocious child that I was, I had him when I was a mere baby, myself.)

Occupation: Writer

Marital Status: Chased, caught, and—very happily—hog-tied for life.

Ideal partner: Someone who gives me room to dream, then encourages me to chase those dreams. Someone who holds me at night, when things look their worst, and tells me everything will work out. Someone who gives great hugs and better kisses. In other words...the man I married.

Strangest date: It's a toss-up. Either the date who took me to see *The Exorcist* and then proposed at a tacky coffee shop afterward. (Shiver!) Or the guy who took me—on our first date, no less—to the San Francisco Academy of Science to see a program on the Sex Changes of Fish. I ditched the first one, married the second. (Hey, it *was* an interesting program and everyone deserves a second chance. Besides the dates *did* improve from there!)

The Nine-Dollar Daddy

Day Leclaire

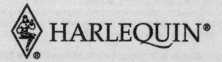

TORONTO • NEW YORK • LONDON
AMSTERDAM • PARIS • SYDNEY • HAMBURG
STOCKHOLM • ATHENS • TOKYO • MILAN • MADRID
PRAGUE • WARSAW • BUDAPEST • AUCKLAND

To Gillian Green, editor extraordinaire,
who came up with the concept for this series
and was generous enough to include me.
Thanks, Gillian!

ISBN 0-373-03543-8

THE NINE-DOLLAR DADDY

First North American Publication 1999.

Copyright © 1999 by Day Totton Smith.

PROLOGUE

"CLASS is dismissed," the teacher announced. "Have a good spring vacation. Oh, and Hutch Lonigan? I'd like to see you before you leave."

Uh-oh. He could tell from her tone that she wasn't happy. A stream of hulking seventh-graders filed out, flicking him quick, amused glances. Of course, they always looked at him that way. As a ten-year-old daring to invade their territory, he was often treated with a mixture of scorn, suspicion and occasionally open dislike.

Stacking his books in a neat pile on his desk, he slipped from his seat and approached Mrs. Roon. "Yes, ma'am?" The teacher shuffled some papers. *She's nervous*, he realized. Okay. Maybe that would work to his advantage. Settling his glasses more firmly on his nose, he fixed her with a cool, direct gaze. That particular look always seemed to bother people. "I hope there isn't anything wrong." He didn't phrase it as a question.

She glanced at him quickly, then away. Flipping open a folder, she thumped her index finger against a neatly printed set of papers. "It's about your proposed science experiment."

Uh-oh. He'd been afraid of that. "Yes?"

"It's… You must admit, it's a bit unorthodox."

Nothing wrong with that. He waited, allowing his silence to weigh on her.

Mrs. Roon cleared her throat, leafing through the papers in his file as though they held the words she so desperately sought. "I'd like you to consider choosing a different subject."

"No."

"Hutch..."

Her voice had softened, grown motherly. He thrust out his chin another inch. He already had one mother. And she *never* used that pitying tone on him. Not ever. "No," he repeated.

"I understand why you want to conduct this experiment. But it's not acceptable. You must see that?"

"It's a logical approach to resolve a problem that no one else has been able to correct."

"Meaning your mother."

"She's not logical." He ticked his points off on his stubby fingers. "She doesn't see the problem. Therefore she's unlikely to attempt a solution. This experiment will remedy that."

"I'm sorry, Hutch. But I can't authorize your project. At least, not without her agreement."

He balled his hands into fists, then realizing how much they gave away, shoved them into his pockets. "*No!* If she knows about it, the results will be compromised."

Mrs. Roon sighed. "I'm afraid my decision's final. Without your mother's written permission, you'll have to choose another project. Even with her permission, I'm not certain I'd approve. It's too...too..." She gave a helpless shrug. "You're an intelligent boy. And it's a sweet, noble thought. But you must see that it's not appropriate?"

She was using that tone again. He pressed his lips tightly together and continued to glare. "Is that your final word?"

"Yes, Hutch. I'm afraid it is." She closed the folder and slid it across her desk toward him. "We're off these next two weeks for spring break. Take that time to choose another project."

"And if I refuse?"

"Then I'll speak to your mother about it."

"You realize you're not giving me any choice."

"I'm sorry," she repeated.

"Me, too," he muttered beneath his breath. "It's been nice working with you, Mrs. Roon."

Picking up the folder, he returned to his desk. He stood and stared at the tidy stack of books, his brain working at a furious rate.

Mrs. Roon wouldn't change her mind and he couldn't risk his mother's finding out about his experiment. With those two premises a given, he analyzed his predicament. In his mind, the problem formed the trunk of a massive tree, the various solutions growing from it into a huge network of crisscrossing branches. It took only a moment to settle on one of the more intriguing choices.

A tiny smile played around his mouth. It was a thin branch, one way off by itself. A very shaky limb indeed. Risky to climb. But the potential results... They far outweighed that risk.

Turning, he took one final look at his teacher. "Thank you, Mrs. Roon. I'll take care of it." Picking up his empty backpack, he settled it over his shoulders.

"I'm glad, Hutch," she said with a huge, relieved smile. "Aren't you taking your books home with you?"

"No need."

She laughed at that, the sound a little too high-pitched. He made most people nervous, though he'd never understood why. Smart must scare some adults—at least when it was a kid being smart.

"I guess not," she said. "You probably have them all memorized anyway."

"Most of them," he agreed, heading for the door. "Goodbye, Mrs. Roon," he added as an afterthought. He didn't look at her again, his mind already busy listing what he'd have to accomplish over the next sixteen days to achieve his goal. It was a daunting agenda. But then, he always did love a good challenge. He closed the schoolroom door with a decisive click.

And finding his mom a husband would undoubtedly be the greatest challenge of all.

CHAPTER ONE

Equipment/Items Required For Experiment:
1. Find perfect man—see ad and check Mom's schedule.
2. Obtain contract/agreement for services.
3. Prepare list for "love" experiments.

HUTCH stopped in the middle of the sidewalk in front of the bright yellow house and stared up at it. Glancing at the newspaper ad, he double-checked the address. Unfortunately, it was correct. The numbers matched. Carefully refolding the ad, he returned it to his back pocket. Jeez. Yellow Rose Matchmakers on Bluebonnet Drive. How corny could you get? Even the picket-fenced house looked silly, all yellow and white with a girly mailbox covered in painted roses. His mother would love it. He hated it. It left him feeling even more out of place than the first time he'd walked into the seventh grade and had everyone eye him as if he was some sort of freak.

Unlatching the white gate, he followed the walkway to the porch steps, stomping up the six wooden risers. Stomping eased his tension. It was a guy thing and doing guy things always helped when you were stuck in a "girl" kind of place. A door barred his entrance, frosted glass preventing him from seeing inside.

Taking a deep breath, he shoved open the door and stepped across the threshold. To his surprise, it didn't seem much like an office at all, but like a real house. The overwhelming scent of flowers made him wrinkle his nose and he grimaced at the cause—a huge floral arrangement perched on a nearby table. Man, how did they stand it? They needed to get some dogs and cats in here to help cut the odor. He peered around, his attention snagged by a desk that occupied a room off the entranceway. Relief surged through him. Desks meant business.

He didn't look left or right, just focused on his goal— the expanse of wood with a nameplate on it that read Receptionist. An old lady stood behind the desk, frowning at a computer printout. Not a good sign. Beside her hovered a man and woman, whispering to each other. The man held a camera while the woman clutched a notepad. They gave him a cursory, dismissive glance. That was okay. He'd gotten used to that sort of reaction.

Setting his jaw, he reached into his pocket and yanked out a fistful of crumpled bills, along with a handful of change. He slapped the money onto the glass-covered top. A quarter rolled toward the old lady, stopping shy of the edge of the desk. It was a whole nine dollars and eighty-four cents. A pitiful amount, but it was his life's savings and he'd worked darned hard to get even that much.

"I want to buy as many dates as I can with this," he announced loudly.

That got everyone's attention. The man and woman stopped whispering and stared at him in sudden, predatory interest. The receptionist put down her computer printout to study him. Eyes as piercing blue as his own fixed on him and one fine white brow arched upward. "Kind of young, aren't you, sonny?"

Warmth bled into his cheeks and he scowled. He didn't like people making fun of him. He got enough of that at school. "It's for my mom. She needs a man and I want the best one you got."

Just like that, her eyes changed. The blue grew as warm and sunny as a hot San Antonio sky. "Do you now?" she murmured. Beside her, a flashbulb went off.

Poking a hand into his back pocket, he came up with the carefully folded ad. He spread it next to his money. He saw the Yellow Rose Matchmakers logo. As always, it cheered him. Yellow roses. It was a good sign. As good an omen as the huge bouquet of yellow roses decorating the old lady's desk. It even made him more tolerant of the stink. "I'd like the San Antonio Fiesta Special. Please," he added as an afterthought.

"Does your mom know you're here?" the woman with the notepad questioned.

"No. It's a birthday present. A *surprise* birthday present."

The receptionist inclined her head. "Oh, I don't doubt it'll be that." For a long moment, she continued to fix him with her intense blue gaze, weighing, examining, scrutinizing. He returned her look boldly. At long last, satisfaction eased her expression and a broad smile slipped across her mouth. She checked the hallway leading to the back of the agency. "Ty?" she called. "I could use your help."

Hutch didn't hear the man approach. One minute the doorway was empty and the next it was overflowing with a huge, broad male. "What's up?" he asked in a voice that rumbled like a distant storm.

"He's my grandson," the old lady explained in an undertone. "He'll take good care of you and your mom."

It required every ounce of determination for Hutch to keep his sneakers planted on the oak floorboards instead of plowing at light speed in the direction of the nearest exit. He hadn't anticipated this!

"I'd appreciate it if you'd do me a favor," she said to Ty, casting a meaningful glance toward the woman with the notepad and the man with the camera. "Maria and Wanda are out to lunch and I'm conducting business. I need you to get this young man started on our San Antonio Fiesta special."

The man's pale green gaze switched from the receptionist to pierce Hutch. "Come again?" he asked softly.

"Help him fill out an application for his mother." Another flashbulb lit up the room. "Please."

"Willie—"

"It's not that hard, Ty." She slapped a multipaged form

onto the desk. "Use my office. Have him answer these questions as best he can. Once you're done, we'll run his mother through the computer and see who we get for a match."

"I need a good one," Hutch inserted determinedly. "The best one in there."

Willie smiled. "I'll make sure of it personally. Go with Ty and he'll help with the forms."

Hutch slid a longing glance toward the door leading to freedom. He could either make a break for it and run on home or he could go with the human mountain. He weighed his choices for an endless nanosecond. Then, settling his glasses more firmly on the bridge of his nose, he nodded at the man. "Let's go," he said.

Ty took the application from Willie and enclosed it in the biggest hand Hutch had ever seen. He checked out the man's feet. Jeez. They were every bit as huge. He'd better be careful where he stood. One misstep and he'd be flatter than an amoeba squashed between glass slides. Without another word of acknowledgment, the man started down the hallway. Hutch trotted cautiously behind.

Opening a door, The Mountain waved the application toward a pair of cushioned chairs set at angles in front of a desk. "Have a seat."

A computer overwhelmed half the broad wooden surface, putting Hutch at his ease. Sidling into the office, he chose the chair closest to the door. His feet dangled ridiculously and he folded them cross-legged beneath him, not caring if his shoes dusted up the cushions. He shot a hard look at the man, daring him to comment. Silence reigned for a full two minutes.

"Why don't you want to help me?" Hutch finally asked.

"I don't work here. I guess you could call me a silent partner."

"Oh." He hadn't offered the expected answer and Hutch took a moment to digest it. "Why did the old lady—"

"Her name's Willie Eden. She's the owner."

"Why'd Miss Willie ask you to help me, then?"

"Like she said, I'm her grandson. I check over the business every so often to make sure it's running smoothly. Today was my checkup day."

"Bummer."

A slow smile built across the man's lean face. "My thoughts exactly."

"What was with the pictures that guy took of me?"

"More bad timing. They're reporters here to do a follow-up story on the agency. I suspect they found you perfect copy."

Hutch couldn't conceal his alarm. "Are they gonna put me in the paper? They can't! This is supposed to be a surprise."

"I'll take care of it."

To his astonishment, Hutch realized he believed the guy. There was something solid and dependable about him. Trustworthy. "So what now?"

"Now we do what Willie said." He frowned down at the application. "We fill out this questionnaire. It might be a bit tricky. A lot of these questions are personal."

"No problem. I know what I—my mom. I know what *my mom* wants." The man's pale green gaze latched onto Hutch again, as cutting and direct as a laser. He'd be a tough man to fool. In fact, Hutch suspected he'd be near impossible to fool. Best to play this part straight. "Okay... To be honest, I wouldn't mind if there was stuff about him I liked, too. I'll need to get along with him, same as Mom."

"Not an easy prospect, I suspect."

The Mountain's gaze continued to cut, burrowing in uncomfortably deep. How much could he see with those odd, piercing eyes? Hutch stirred nervously. "I won't be too picky, if that's what's worrying you. I can't afford to be." To his relief, the gaze eased enough for him to breathe a little better.

"What's your name, boy?"

"Hutch Lonigan. And before you bother asking, I'm ten."

"Ty Merrick. I'm thirty-one. Now that we're clear where we stand, why don't we get down to business." He picked up a pen. "What's your mother's name?"

"Cassidy Lonigan."

"Address and phone."

Hutch reluctantly supplied it. "But you're not gonna call her, are you?"

"That's up to Willie." That slow smile appeared again. "I'm just following orders today, remember?"

"Okay, I guess."

"What's your mom's age?"

"Old. That's why we have to get this taken care of fast." Ty's smile grew. "Don't suppose she's told you how old?"

"She's gonna be twenty-nine tomorrow. That means she doesn't have much time left. Jeez! She's already got her first couple of wrinkles." He gestured toward the corner of his eyes. "Before you know it, she's gonna be a total prune."

"Going downhill fast. Got it."

"Don't write that down!" Hutch considered a way around the problem. "Maybe if they go somewhere dark, her date won't notice. Write down that she likes romantic settings. They're dark, right? Movies and candlelight and stuff?"

Ty disappeared behind the form. "Good suggestion, kid. I'll make a note of it." His rumbling voice sounded oddly choked and the papers rustled. But a moment later, he lowered the form, looking as mountainlike as ever. "Next. Height and weight. Do you have a clue about those?"

"She's not fat. I guess she's okay in that department. And she's pretty tall for a girl. Bigger'n me," he added beneath his breath.

Of course, Ty heard. "Give yourself a chance, kid. Male

hormones tend to kick in later than women's. And she's got a whole passel of years on you."

"I know. It's straight genetics." His chin inched out and he tried to tuck it back in. By Ty's expression, his attempt hadn't met with much success. "Either I got the height gene or I didn't. Since tall is a dominant trait, chances are in my favor that I'll shoot up one of these days."

"Then there's not much point in worrying about it, is there?" came the cool response. "Hair and eye color?"

"Brown and gray."

"I assume it's her hair that's brown and her eyes that are gray?"

For the first time, Hutch felt the urge to laugh. It escaped as a tiny snort. "Yeah."

"What a relief." An answering grin flickered across Ty's face.

"Wanna see a picture?"

"Sure."

Hutch dug the photo from his pocket and handed it over, hiding a smirk at the mountain man's reaction. Ty's expression was sorta the way Hutch's got over a big bowl of ice cream. Course, his mom was a lot better than ice cream. Even the kids at school thought so. If they had a contest for best-looking mom, he'd win hands down.

Without a word, Ty returned the photo and picked up the application form again. "Occupation?"

Hutch frowned in thought. "I think she's a waitress this week."

"This week?"

"She takes what she can get, okay? She works really hard. It's not like she has a husband or anything to help pay the bills."

Ty held up his hands—long-fingered, hard-worn hands. Hands like his mom's, only a lot bigger. It helped ease Hutch's distress to see the evidence of a man branded by work. "Easy, buster. I'm just asking the questions on the application. I'm not judging. Got it?"

Hutch nodded, aware he'd revealed too much of himself to this man. He'd have to watch that. "What else do you need to know?"

"Marital status. Children. Type of residence."

Hutch took a deep breath. "We live in an apartment. She's single. Lonnie—he was my dad—took off five years ago." He shrugged. "I guess I shoulda said divorced. The papers came through a while after he left. As for children...I'm it. So the guy won't have to worry about having any sniveling brats around. It's just the two of us and I won't give him any trouble."

Ty lowered his gaze at the telling comments. "I'm sure you won't." Poor kid. Calling his father by his given name. Did he realize how desperate he sounded to find a replacement? Doubtful. The boy had it all figured out...or thought he did.

"Okay. What's the next question?" Hutch demanded.

Ty flipped to the second page. "What would her ideal partner be like? Any idea?"

"A cowboy."

"Come again?"

"Or a rancher."

"You're kidding."

"Well, it's the only kind she hasn't tried yet."

Uh-oh. "Tried?"

"Yeah. Places we've lived and stuff."

Ty tapped his pen against the application form. It was the "and stuff" that bothered him. Did Hutch mean that the way it sounded? Had his mother tried out various types of men, seeking the perfect partner? Ty's mouth tightened. For some reason, it bothered him to consider that possibility, especially after seeing Cassidy Lonigan's wide, generous smile and the hint of vulnerability peeking from big gray eyes. "You move around a lot?"

"Have to. At first we were keeping up with Lonnie. Now Mom's trying to find us the perfect home."

To go with her perfect man? "I gather she hasn't found it yet?"

"Nope. That's why I decided to help. Her way isn't working."

"And you think this will?"

"You use that computer sittin' there, don't you?" At Ty's agreement, Hutch nodded in satisfaction. "Then it'll work. Now, what else do you need to know?"

Deciding a change of subject was in order, Ty asked, "Does she have any pet peeves?"

"April Mae."

"Excuse me?"

"That's the girl my dad ran off with. April Mae. Lonnie had to wait until she graduated from high school before leaving us and that peeved Mom a whole lot. I don't think the guy you pick oughta mention her cuz Mom'll have a thing or two to say on the subject. And none of it'll be good."

"I imagine."

"Is that it? Are we finished?"

"Not quite." Ty frowned, running a hand across his jawline. He didn't like having the boy answer these questions. They'd already discussed some pretty intimate issues. Unfortunately, it was about to get a whole hell of a lot more intimate. "Now for the tough part."

Hutch practically shot off the chair. "You're kidding! You mean all those other questions were supposed to be easy?"

Ty offered a sympathetic smile. "'Fraid so. It gets a little more personal from here."

"*More* personal? What else can they want to know? You mean like...like..." An expression of abject horror crept across Hutch's face. "No way! That's disgusting. My mom doesn't *do* that sorta stuff."

Ty buried his amusement. She had to have done it at one point or another since the evidence sat glaring straight at him. Not that he'd mention that small detail to Hutch. He was a smart kid. It would occur to him in time. "You know…this would be easier if we could get her input. You sure you can't bring her here for her birthday? We could ask all these questions and get a better sense—"

"No! She won't do it if—" Hutch broke off, his face reddening.

Ty's amusement faded. "Please. Don't stop there. You don't think she'd agree if she knew what you were up to?" Great. Just what his grandmother needed. More trouble. He leaned across the desk, shoving a bud vase aside. The single yellow rose it contained trembled at the rough treatment. "Look, kid. If it's not something she wants, why give it to her?"

The boy's youthful chin jutted out again and Ty released his breath in a slow sigh. If the kid wasn't careful, someone would take that jaw as a challenge and peg it with a fist. Not that Hutch would give up. He was a scrapper. Too bad he didn't have the size to back his attitude. It would save him a few hard knocks.

"She may not want it," Hutch announced, "but she's gonna get it anyway."

"I'm sure she'll appreciate that." The boy flushed at Ty's dry tone. "Face facts, kid. If you aren't able to answer the questions, I can't run her profile. So either you answer or she does. Which is it going to be?"

Hutch's face screwed up in distaste. "Oh, man. This is *not* good. What other questions are there?"

Ty glanced at the form. "Strengths, weaknesses, general interests and hobbies. Personality type. Goals and ambitions. And then she's supposed to describe herself." The boy appeared nonplussed. A first, Ty was willing to bet.

"Well, shoot…" Hutch released a gusty breath, his bewilderment rapidly dissipating. "Okay. Does your phone have a hold or mute button?"

Ty checked. "Both."

"And does it have a speaker button?"

"Yes."

"Perfect. May I use it for a sec?"

Ty shoved the phone across the desk. "Be my guest."

Picking up the receiver, Hutch rapidly punched in a series of numbers. "Hey, Mom? It's me. You on your way to work?" He waited a moment, listening. "Oh, good. I'm putting you on speaker, okay?"

Hutch stabbed a button and a voice sweeter than a honey-coated Georgia peach filled the room. "...sweetpea, I don't mind."

"You're not supposed to call me that, remember?"

"Sorry, sweet—Hutch. So what's up? Where are you?"

"I'm at a friend's house and need some help. I'm working on a science project for school and—"

"A friend?" The excitement in her voice was painfully apparent, lacing the words with a warmer, heavier note of maternal concern. "Have I met him? Or is it a her?"

"Him. No, you haven't met. About this project—"

"What's his name?"

Hutch exhaled noisily. "His name is Ty Merrick. Mom. Pay attention. This is important."

"I'm sorry, sweet—Hutch. How can I help?"

"We're doing a personality survey for this science experiment and I need to ask you a bunch of questions."

"Oh..." There was a momentary pause. "Will anyone realize it's me?"

"It's confidential," Ty murmured to Hutch.

"Is that you, Ty? Gracious. You sound all grown up."

Hutch started. "The kids in my class are a lot older than me, Mom. You know that. Ty's...really big."

"Oh, dear. Was I being rude? Sorry about that, Ty. I hope I didn't embarrass you."

His name came across the phone line as warm and gentle as a sigh. The way she said "Tah" wrapped around him. It wasn't a Texas accent. Perhaps he'd been more accurate about that Georgia peach than he realized. Suddenly, he had the urge to meet a leggy twenty-nine-year-old with brown hair just a shade shy of black and gray eyes that

shone like silver. To see if up close and personal the eyes—
with the tiny wrinkles in the corners that Hutch found so
disturbing—were as intensely appealing as her voice.

Apparently, he'd waited too long to respond. Her breath
caught and she said, "I did embarrass you. I'm *so* sorry,
Ty. I didn't mean—"

"You didn't embarrass me." It took an instant for the
soft reassurance to reach her—soft, so she wouldn't realize
he was a man, not a child. "I was trying to figure out where
your accent was from."

"Oh." Sunshine filled her voice, breaking through the
clouds of uncertainty. "I'm from the good ol' goober state
of Georgia."

"Goober?" he questioned, intrigued.

She chuckled, and a picture of her generous smile filled
his mind. Darn that photo! One look and he'd been a goner.
"That's what they call peanuts back there. We might be
the Empire State, but we're really a bunch of goobers."

Hutch stirred. "Mom. Can we ask you questions? Do
you mind?"

"Not at all. Fire away, sugar."

"Okay. I'm gonna put you on hold for a sec so me and
Ty can pick the questions."

She laughed. "You don't want to discuss them in front
of me?"

"Can't. It might corrupt the results."

Her laughter blossomed, as rich and smooth as her voice.
Ty clenched his jaw against the sound, not quite believing
the effect it was having on him. "We can't allow that, now
can we? Go ahead and talk. I'll wait."

"Thanks, Mom." Hutch stabbed the hold button and
frowned at Ty. "You almost gave it away."

"I don't like deceiving people. Next time don't rope me
in to your lie. I won't tolerate it. Are we clear about that?"

Abashed, Hutch nodded. "Yes, sir. Sorry."

Ty gave him a stern look. "Okay. Let's get this done."
He tossed a list of character traits across the desk toward

the boy. "I need some idea of what she considers her personality type. Read your mom the list and have her choose the ones that best describe her."

Hutch frowned at the sheet. "I could probably figure these out."

"It's better if she did it."

Apparently, Hutch agreed because he leaned forward and punched the hold button. "You there, Mom?"

"Right here."

"Okay. I'm going to read off a list of personality traits and you pick the ones that fit you best. Got it?"

"I think I can handle that." By the subtle amusement coloring her words, Ty suspected she was well accustomed to Hutch's high-handedness. As soon as her son finished rattling off the list, she said, "You can definitely mark me down as sentimental and affectionate. I tend to be huggy," she confessed, probably for his sake, Ty realized.

"*Real* huggy," Hutch inserted.

"I also consider myself extroverted. I like jobs that bring me in contact with people. And I'm pretty self-assured. I'm going to do what I think best, regardless of anyone else's opinion." She hesitated. "What else hits home? I guess you could call me adventurous, since we move around so much. But romantic is definitely out."

"Aw, come on, Mom. What about all those smelly bubble baths and candles? Those are romantic."

"Those, my poor misguided son, are feminine, not romantic. I can enjoy 'girl stuff', as you like to call it, without having it involve a man or romance. It's for my own pleasure, not to entice a husband."

Ty shot Hutch a disgruntled look. Obviously the woman had been badly burned by her ex. Chances were excellent that she wasn't the least interested in the services the Yellow Rose had to offer. Just his luck. And just Willie's luck, too. What the hell were they going to tell the reporters if Cassidy refused to cooperate? "Remind me to wring your

neck when we're done here," he told the boy in an undertone.

A hint of red crept into Hutch's cheeks, but other than
that one telling sign, he acted as though he hadn't heard.
"Go on, Mom. Any others?"

"Let's see.... I'm tolerant, practical—"

"No way."

"Sure I am, Hutch." Utter bewilderment laced her voice.
"Why would you think I'm not practical?"

Hutch snorted. "If you were practical, you wouldn't
keep givin' stuff away. You wouldn't let our landlady help
herself to clippings off your rosebushes any time the mood
took her. And you woulda sued Lonnie when he stole all
our money and ran off with April Mae in your new pickup.
She's not practical," Hutch repeated to Ty. Otherwise he
wouldn't be sitting here finding her a date, his tone added.

"I sure wish your daddy hadn't done that," she admitted
in a low voice. "I'm afraid it set a bad example. And it
left hard feelings between the two of you."

Cassidy's simple observation threatened to rip through
Ty's callused hide. It came across as unbearably painful.
He had to get this show on the road and this kid on his
way. Fast. Before he formed an attachment to a honey-
warm voice and a prickly ten-year-old brainiac. He punched
the hold button before Hutch could get to it. "Let's move
this along, kid. And stop coloring the results. Just ask the
questions, let her answer them and move on to the next.
Got it?"

"Yeah. I got it." Hutch sounded as subdued as his
mother. "And so's you know... It wasn't Lonnie's running
off that left hard feelings. It was what he said on his way
out the door. He hasn't called since he took off and..."
The chin wobbled for a telling instant. "And he made Mom
cry. The next guy she marries isn't gonna do that. He's
gonna make her laugh."

Ty stirred, suffering from a nasty case of empathy. The
kid just wanted his mother to be happy. Too bad he thought

a man could do that for her. "Look, boy," he said gently, "you don't find happiness by getting married. You find it inside yourself first and then share it with others. Sometimes through marriage. And sometimes through friendship."

Hutch folded his arms tight across his narrow chest. "You sound like my mom."

That didn't surprise him. Cassidy sounded like a level-headed woman—unlike her stubborn son. "Maybe you ought to listen to her."

"Maybe," the boy muttered. "What's the next question?"

Ty scanned the page. Damn. "I'll read off this particular bunch, if you don't mind."

"Okay."

"And you're not going to interrupt?"

Hutch shrugged. "Not unless she gets it wrong."

Ty bit back his response and punched the hold button. "Ms. Lonigan?"

"Still here, Ty." To his relief, she sounded a lot more chipper.

"These next few are going to be a bit personal. Just answer them the best you're able."

"Go ahead."

"What's your favorite way to spend an evening?" He found himself unexpectedly curious to hear the answer.

"That's an easy one," Cassidy replied. "I'd spend it in a hot, scented bubble bath with a bunch of those stinky candles Hutch hates so much. Oh! And a good book."

Ty blinked at the image his mind created, the fantasy made easy thanks to one slightly creased photo. He pictured mounds of frothy bubbles clinging to white silky skin and dark hair piled on top of her head, with damp strands surrounding a piquant face. Huge, somber gray eyes with a hint of mischief sparkling in their depths would peek at him from the middle of the tub. And candlelight would catch in the bubbles and play across her shoulders, emphasizing the purity of her skin. He'd swipe a speck of foam from the tip of her upturned nose before leaning down to—

"Is that all your questions?" Cassidy interrupted.

Ty snatched up the application. *Keep your mind on business, son!* "Sorry. I have a few more. What are your strengths and weaknesses?"

"Boy, those are tough ones. I guess I'd say I'm a hard worker." She'd probably had to be, Ty acknowledged. "As for weaknesses…"

"You're too generous," Hutch spoke up.

"That's not a weakness, sugar." There was a brief pause and then she sighed. "To be perfectly honest, I guess I'm too darn proud. I want to take care of myself and Hutch so I don't have to depend on anyone ever again. Whatever I need, I plan to get for myself."

Ty considered her comment. No doubt her ex had a lot to do with her attitude. He could understand that. Cassidy Lonigan reminded him of Willie—a strong, determined woman, chock-full of passion and energy. He smiled. Hell, she should have been a Texan born and bred. She'd fit right in. "Next question. What's your idea of a perfect date?"

"Goodness, that's an odd one," she said with a trace of uncertainty. "You said this is for a science project?"

"Yes," Hutch injected hastily. "I'll explain it to you after it's done."

"Well…I guess a perfect date would be yellow roses and food." Her laugh eased across the line, stirring an odd sensation deep in Ty's gut. He could almost see her face light up, her expression filled with humor and spirit and character. "So long as you feed me, I'm happy."

"And the yellow roses?"

"I like them. They're…hopeful."

"She's got a thing for them," Hutch whispered. "That's why I picked this place."

"Makes sense," Ty muttered. At least, as much sense as any of this made.

"Listen, boys, I have to get ready for work. Are we almost finished here?"

"Just one more question," Ty said. "What are your goals and ambitions?"

"To raise my son the best I can," Cassidy answered promptly. "I'm saving to buy a house of our very own. A small place with a yard and a garden where I can plant yellow roses. A home where we can set down roots nice and deep. The permanent kind."

Ty understood all about roots. His family had lived in the San Antonio area for generations. The homestead he owned had been his father's and his father's before him— a long line of Merricks stretching into the past, their history and heritage planted so deep in Texas soil, they could never be yanked free. "Roots are good," he agreed.

"I'm glad you think so, Ty. That's my goal. To have a home, my roses, and most important of all, my family close by. I don't want or need another blessed thing beside that."

"Not even a husband?" he suggested.

"Gracious, no! *Especially* not a husband. What put that crazy idea in your head?"

Her vehement response exploded in the room. For a long moment, Ty sat quietly in his chair, struggling to control his temper. "I haven't a clue," he answered through gritted teeth. Heaven help him, he was going to kill the kid. Maybe he could step on him and claim he'd squashed the boy by mistake. "Thanks, Ms. Lonigan. I appreciate your taking the time to talk to us."

"You're certainly welcome. Hutch? When will you be home?"

"I'll be back in time for dinner, Mom." His voice held a nervous squeak that, fortunately, his mother didn't hear.

"Call if you're going to be late. And feel free to invite Ty if you'd like."

The instant the connection was broken, Ty leaned across the desk toward the boy. "Definitely not a husband?" he questioned softly. "*Definitely not?*"

Hutch waved a dismissive hand. "It's a temporary fixation. She has this thing about being independent right now. I'll take care of it." A nervous bravado crept into his expression. "How come you stopped the interview? That wasn't all the questions."

"Aside from the fact that it's an exercise in futility?"

Hutch cleared his throat. "Yeah. Aside from that."

"The last one would have tipped our hand, which might be for the best, all things considered."

"No! I—"

"So, you'll have to answer it," Ty cut in. "Assuming we're continuing with this nonsense."

"I'm still sittin' here, aren't I?" Before Ty could argue that particular assertion, Hutch asked, "Okay, what's the last one?"

As pointless as the final question seemed, it would complete the damned form and get this mule-headed kid on his way. "What do you think your mother is seeking in a relationship?"

"What do you mean?"

"What does she want from the guy she dates?"

"Oh. That's easy." Hutch offered an endearing grin. "You can tell she doesn't know it yet. But she wants marriage."

OPERATION HUSBAND
by Hutch Lonigan
Progress Report

The Mountain wasn't very happy with me. Said I was keeping secrets and better cut it out. Well...yeah, I'm keeping secrets! How else am I going to get a dad? Anyway, he promised to have a man available for Mom by tomorrow for her birthday. Once that happens I can get the experiment going. The computer better pick a good one. I might not get another shot at this. I still have to set things up at school and may have to put Plan B into action. Hope not. But Mom comes first! And since she won't take care of this herself...somebody's got to take charge.

Looks like I'm it.

CHAPTER TWO

Equipment and Procedures to Organize:
1. Take Mom to Yellow Rose Matchmakers without her
catching on.
2. Have the computer do its magic.
3. Check the stats on the match. (Note: Make sure this
guy's not a loser.)
4. Convince Mom to go along with it. (Sure wish wishes
were scientific!)

CASSIDY calculated the figures for the fourth time. Not that
it changed anything. The bottom line on her checking-
account register still added up to the same pitiful amount
as before—an amount too small to meet all her current
financial demands. She clenched her fingers around the tiny
nub of a pencil her boss, Freddie, had been wasteful enough
to trash, her knuckles turning white from the strain. What
the heck was she going to do?

A lock of thick, dark brown hair drifted into her eyes
and she pushed it away with hands that trembled. Darn it
all! Why couldn't she have curls instead of hair so painfully
straight not even a rubber band would hold it? At least curls
could be confined or cropped short. At least curls would—
Stop it, she ordered herself briskly. *Stop wasting time on*
foolishness and focus on the serious problems. There were
certainly enough of them to keep her occupied.

She scowled at the check register again. Okay. The final
payment on Hutch's computer would come first, she decided. It had to. That computer was his future. She tapped
the pencil on the scarred kitchen table. And maybe if she
spoke to Mrs. Walters, explained that she'd pick up an extra

shift or two and get the money together by the end of the week, the landlady would let the rent slide a few more days. She might...especially if Cassidy bribed her with another clipping from her poor rosebushes.

Okay, what next? The utilities. She'd dole out a few precious dollars on her electric bill. That way, the computer would have a place to live and the juice to run it. Let's see...next on the list would have to be food. She perked up a bit. Perhaps Freddie would have some leftovers from the restaurant she could take home. That might help stretch their pennies. And she could give up all the extras. No more instant coffee. Skip the odd lunch. Tape up the hole in her sneaker. Not get sick or twist any more ankles. She could get by. Sure she—

"Everything okay, Mom?"

She glued a bright smile on her face. "Just fine, sweetie. Why?"

Hutch perched on the edge of the chair across from her. "Your eyes are that funny color again."

She stared at him in bewilderment. "What funny color?"

"Like pencil lead." He glanced at the open check register. "What's wrong?"

"Nothing. Everything's great." He didn't believe her, not that his skepticism surprised her. He often saw things no one else noticed. "Really," she insisted, "we're fine."

"I can tell if there's something wrong," he explained patiently. "When you laugh, your eyes are a pretty silver. But when you're upset, they look like lead. So, what's wrong?"

"Oh." Crud. "I hadn't realized."

Smile! she ordered herself sternly. *Think of something happy*. She forcibly summoned a picture of Hutch right after she'd given birth to him. Even then, he'd displayed an intense curiosity that was such an innate part of his character. He'd peered up at her with huge blue eyes and she'd known in that instant that she'd do anything for him...sacrifice anything. He'd been the one bright spot in

months of fear and desperation. He'd made everything
worthwhile and just thinking about him eased her tension.

Cassidy smiled. "How's that?"

"Hey! They're silver again."

"It must have been the light," she teased.

"I guess." He kicked the table leg. "You won't forget
about tomorrow, right? You need to get off work for a
couple of hours so I can take you for your birthday surprise."

She frowned, fingering the checkbook. "I don't know,
Hutch...."

"You promised, Mom. Please."

"And a promise is a promise," she conceded with a sigh.
"Okay, sweetpea. I'll talk to Freddie." And to Mrs.
Walters. And to the electric company. They'd all understand. She drew an anxious breath. There wasn't any
choice. They had to.

"He wants a father."

Willie nodded. "Most boys do, Ty. Is that so bad?"

Ty unhitched his shoulder from the support pillar he'd
been leaning against and turned to face his grandmother.
She sat at the far end of the porch in a large wooden swing,
her favorite spot at the Yellow Rose to "ruminate" as she
called it. "Not for Hutch. But I doubt Cassidy feels the
same way. She sounded as though she'd had her fill of
men." An understatement if ever he'd uttered one. "What
if she kicks up a fuss because we've encouraged this kid's
scheme?"

"Is that the impression she gave when you spoke? Did
she seem like a troublemaker?"

Ty frowned. No. He'd sensed Cassidy Lonigan was a
warmhearted woman devoted to her son—a woman thrilled
to her tippytoes that Hutch had a friend. A friend she'd
immediately invited over for dinner. "She'll date whom-
ever the computer picks. She won't like it, but she'll do it
for the boy."

"There you are, then. Problem solved."

"It's not solved, Willie." He frowned, not quite sure why he was involving himself in the Lonigan match. He had more than enough work waiting at the ranch. Nice, strenuous, mind-numbing jobs. The sort that didn't leave room for thoughts of Georgia peaches and porcupine boys. But Willie had raised him from the time he was a snot-nosed whelp. He owed her more than he could ever hope to repay. Investing in her company and checking up on her business interests periodically was a small way of showing his appreciation. "Is it wise to encourage this kid's scheme when it's clear his mother isn't interested?"

"Perhaps she'll discover the man of her dreams," Willie replied complacently, setting the porch swing in motion. "That *is* what we do, Ty."

He released his breath in a gusty sigh. "You've been borrowing Wanda's rose-tinted glasses, haven't you? I hate when you do that."

Willie chuckled. "Don't pick on Wanda. She's the best employee I have."

"That's open to debate."

"Just because she's a romantic—"

"That's not the objection I have to her and you darn well know it."

Willie brushed that aside. "It's not like we don't have a few romantic legends in our own family."

"Don't start that again," he warned.

"You're the most hardheaded man I know." Her snowy brows drew together, signaling her annoyance. "Do you really think I'd have told you about The Kiss if I didn't believe in it myself? What do you take me for? Some doddering old half-witted fool?"

"Yup." He joined his grandmother on the swing and slung an arm around her shoulders, plying her with the sense of humor he'd inherited from the Eden branch of the family. "I suspect you're one step away from a padded room with a beefy guard named Louie."

Willie clicked her tongue in exasperation. "Oh, go on with you. I'm serious. Because you haven't kissed the right woman yet doesn't mean she isn't out there wondering what the heckfire's keeping you."

"You've been feeding me this story since I was a baby," he objected. "When are you going to give it up?"

"Never! It was as true for your parents as it was for your grandfather and me. Just as it was true for his parents before him, and his before that. Mark my words. It'll happen to you, too."

Ty bit off a laugh. "One kiss and I'll know."

"Whether it's true love." She gave an adamant nod. "Yes, sir, you will. It's taking you a bit longer than it did the rest of us is all."

"I believe we were discussing Cassidy Lonigan's love life. Why don't we focus on that and keep me out of it?" He didn't wait for her to agree—which was probably just as well since it looked as though agreeing with him was the last thing likely to escape the sharp edge of her tongue. "That reporter's still sniffing around, isn't she?"

"She was...intrigued by young Hutch. She was particularly intrigued by the fact that we let him buy a date for only nine dollars."

Ty didn't like the sound of that. "She didn't think you were doing it as a publicity stunt, did she? I'd be happy to clarify the matter for her."

Willie waved off his concern. "Yes, the question was raised. And I believe Maria set the woman straight in short order."

Somewhat appeased, Ty asked, "So this reporter's going to follow up on the dates the Yellow Rose arranges?"

Willie shrugged. "Probably."

"And when nothing good comes from it? What if Cassidy rejects the candidates the computer chooses?"

"Why don't we worry about that if it happens?"

Something in his grandmother's tone had him fixing her with a sharp-eyed gaze. She sounded almost...complacent.

That had to mean trouble. "Why don't we worry about it now. Perhaps we can come up with some alternate ideas if the worst happens."

"You're such a pessimist, Ty."

"I'm realistic. Cassidy Lonigan had one bad marriage. From what the boy said, she's tried various other relationships without any success. So he's decided to take a hand in matters. That's not a formula guaranteed to yield positive results."

"Stop being so logical," Willie groused. "You're thinking with your head—"

"I certainly hope so."

"Yes, well, it's her heart we're concerned with, isn't it? That's what we've been hired to engage. Why don't you give the agency a chance before deciding it won't work?"

"Maybe I'd be more willing to go along if it wasn't for last month's foul-up. Does that ring a bell? When your dear employee kept matching everyone all by her lonesome? Wanda didn't even have the computer—" He broke off with a frown. "What did she call it?"

"George."

"She didn't even have *George* plugged in."

"Her success rate was phenomenal. You can't argue with that."

"Great, except for one small problem. Yellow Rose Matchmakers is billed as a *computerized* dating agency, remember?"

Willie dismissed that with another wave of her hand. "Minor details. The bottom line is…the agency made the matches and they all ended in matrimony. What makes you think this one won't?"

Ty's memory replayed a slow, husky Georgia drawl, the kind that slid all over a man before seeping deep inside. The kind that went with sultry nights, a large bed and hours of hot, sweet loving. "I gather the lady is running scared."

"Then we'll have to be certain we pick someone who'll break her in gently, won't we?"

Ty's mouth twitched. "You make her sound like a horse."

Willie nodded. "In a way, I suspect she's a lot like a mare who's had a rough first ride. It's our job to make sure her next experience is more satisfactory."

"Wrong."

"Wrong?" Her eyebrows winged upward. "How's that, boy?"

He leaned forward and planted a kiss on her tanned cheek. "Making sure her next dating experience is satisfactory is *your* job, not *ours*."

Willie simply smiled. "We'll see."

"Careful, Mom. Don't peek."

"Oh, Hutch. I'm going to trip. Is this blindfold *really* necessary?"

"I want it to be a surprise. And it won't be if you peek."

Cassidy chuckled. "I won't look, I promise. But you'll have to steer me. If I fall and break a leg, I won't be much good as a waitress." The words had barely escaped when her size ten sneakers tangled. "Dagnab it!"

Hutch helped prop her up. "Easy does it. I won't let you fall. Now stand here for a minute while I open the gate."

"There's a gate?"

She tried to catch a glimpse of where they were headed from beneath the voluminous bandanna that served as a blindfold. Not that she wanted to spoil Hutch's surprise. But she'd been wearing the darned thing ever since they'd gotten off the bus a few blocks back. It seemed a wise precaution to make sure she wasn't about to stumble over her own two feet again. With her luck, she'd end up having all five feet eight inches sprawled in a jumbled heap of arms and legs across a painfully hard sidewalk.

She wrinkled her nose a couple of times hoping it might edge the bandanna up a bit, but it remained stubbornly in place. Her son had tied the blindfold with the same thoroughness he gave most of his endeavors.

"Don't bother. I made it tight."

"Come on, sweetpea," she said with a sigh. "Stop teasing. Where are we?"

"At your birthday present. Okay. Now, here come some steps. Put your hand on the banister. That's it. And hold on to me with your other hand. One more step and we'll be on the porch."

An atypical nervousness assailed her. If she'd considered herself the least bit psychic, she'd have thought something momentous was about to occur. Of course, she no longer indulged in such foolish fantasies. She'd learned that painful lesson years ago. "Whose house is this?"

"Not telling. Just stand there while I open the door."

"We can walk right in?" Her concern increased.

"Yup. They know me here." He helped her inside, then released her arm. "You wait by the flowers while I go get Miss Willie."

Cassidy heard the squeak of the door closing behind her, followed by a familiar, rumbly voice addressing Hutch. Where had she heard that distinctive intonation before? she wondered. A customer? A fellow tenant? A teacher? Instead of waiting for her son's return, she took a hesitant step forward and promptly tripped again. Strong arms closed around her—definitely not Hutch's arms. He swept her upward and the bandanna caught on his shirt button, slipping downward a fraction of an inch. The narrow gap afforded her a tantalizing glimpse of the man who held her.

He was impressively large, formed along the same lines as Texas—broad, bold and built to last. Taut sinew and lean, powerful muscles rippled along the ridged biceps beneath her palms as well as across the chest she was practically nuzzling. She dug her nose out of its resting place, but not before a clean, earthy scent filled her nostrils. Heavens to Betsy, but as they'd say back home...the man had a nice stink hanging on him.

He wasn't as handsome as Hutch's dad, Cassidy conceded. But then, Lonnie's good looks had only served to disguise the shallow person beneath. This man's features were blunt and distinctive, drawn with strong, sweeping lines. No question. He was all man, while Lonnie had been a boy when they'd first met and a boy when they'd last parted.

Easing her gaze upward, she found herself staring into the most intriguing pale green eyes she'd ever seen. They gathered her up, impaling her as they dug down deep—searching for a clue to the self she kept tucked safely away. *Slipping clear to her soul*, came the disconcerting thought.

Not safe, a warning voice rang in her head.

She instantly overreacted, a regrettable personality failing she'd yet to correct. She wriggled from the man's arms with more speed than grace, flailing for a brief instant as she fought to keep her limbs from tangling again. "Oops! Don't tell Hutch I saw!" she whispered hastily, yanking her blindfold into place.

She took another quick step backward, filled with an odd urgency to put as much distance between them as possible. She stumbled once more, still not quite secure in her footing. Instantly, his hand closed around her arm and she sensed the latent strength behind his hold.

"Are you okay?" he asked.

Not safe, the warning voice shrieked—louder, in case she hadn't heard clearly the first time.

"Oh, hush up," she muttered in exasperation.

She never listened to those smart-alecky inner voices anymore. They always got it wrong, starting with the time they told her going to bed with Lonnie was a good idea and ending on the day they urged her to fight April Mae for the "honor" of keeping her selfish jerk of a husband. After that disastrous occasion, she realized these were *dumb* inner voices instead of the clever, instinctive ones most people got, so she'd refused to listen further. Not that *they'd* stopped handing out bad advice.

"Excuse me?" Mr. Rumbly Voice said.

Oops. "Sorry. I wasn't talking to you. I was having a small personal argument."

"Uh-huh. You do that a lot?"

"No," she lied cautiously. "I was just arguing with myself. *Everybody* does it." She swept her arm through the air to indicate a whole horde of everybodies. The back of her hand connected with a resounding crack. Carefully, she lowered her arm and grabbed a gulp of air. When would she learn to keep her various body parts under control? "That was you, huh?"

"Yeah. That was me."

She swallowed at the tight tone. "Sorry about that. Sometimes I forget that I'm longer than I feel." She lowered a corner of the blindfold an inch, wincing at the bright red mark on Rumbly Voice's cheek. "You see, I always wanted to be small and dainty. So in my head, my reach is only about twenty-two or -three inches instead of—" She broke off at his incredulous expression.

"Oh, please," he insisted, "don't stop there."

Cassidy sighed. Why did people always look at her like she was crazy when she explained this? False body images were very common. They also caused a person to be a bit of a klutz, a fact she went out of her way to demonstrate with disgusting regularity. She cleared her throat. "I forget my reach is twenty-six inches instead of twenty-three. It's those extra three inches that hit you."

"I see. In that case, I'll make sure I stay clear of them."

And stay clear of you, he might as well have said. Like she hadn't already realized that. "Don't worry. I'll save you the trouble." She yanked the blindfold back into place. "Hutch?" she called. "Where are you, sweetpea?"

"Right here, Mom. Bring her in," Hutch added, apparently addressing ol' Rumbly Voice. "Willie's ready to run the form."

"What's going on?" she demanded.

"Relax, Ms. Lonigan."

Probably afraid if she tensed up, she'd haul off and slug

him again. A distinct possibility, she wanted to warn. All her life she'd struggled to project the image of a graceful Southern belle, like her Aunt Esther. To be small, dainty and gardenia sweet. To her dismay, she'd ended up tall and klutzy, with an unfortunate tendency to speak her mind, forgetting more often than not to lace it with the prerequisite honey. No steel magnolia was she. But, oh, how she longed to be.

"I'm relaxed," she assured him. "But I wouldn't object if you explained what's going on around here."

"Hutch has gone to a lot of trouble to set up this little surprise. I'm sure you don't want to spoil it."

She caught the subtle warning at the exact same instant she recalled where she'd heard those deep, earthy tones before. Lord, she hoped she was wrong. "Ty?" she murmured apprehensively.

"At your service."

Oh, crud. "I...I thought you were a friend of Hutch's."

"I am."

Double crud. "But he told me... I thought—"

"That I was a kid. Sorry about that."

He slid his hands behind her head and she kept carefully still. More than anything, she wanted to bolt. Instead, she held her ground, refusing to give in to ridiculous fears—not to mention a totally unwarranted attraction. She sniffed. It had to be his scent she found enticing because there sure wasn't much else she found attractive. Well...other than his size and interesting eye color. Oh! And his voice. She had a weak spot for deep, rich voices. "What are you doing, if you don't mind my asking?"

"I think we can dispense with this now," he replied, sweeping the blindfold from her face.

Now that she knew his identity, she couldn't resist staring at Ty. He was supposed to be a boy. He was supposed to be a friend of Hutch's. Instead, he was blatantly male. Uncomfortably male. Thoroughly male. And he knew more about the intimate details of her life than any man of recent acquaintance.

"Surprise, Mom," Hutch announced, drawing her attention. "Happy birthday!"

Relieved, she edged closer to her son. "What's up?" she questioned lightly.

For the first time, she realized there were others in the room besides her son and Ty. Next to Hutch stood a handsome, white-haired woman. Something about her bearing and looks suggesting a familial relationship with Ty. And off to one side hovered a man and woman, both watching her with uncomfortable intensity.

The older woman stepped forward and offered her hand. "Welcome, Ms. Lonigan. I'm Willie Eden, owner of Yellow Rose Matchmakers. Your son has purchased our services for your birthday present."

Uh-oh. "What services?" Cassidy asked, fighting to conceal her apprehension.

"We're a dating agency."

Damn. She pasted a delighted smile on her mouth, praying Hutch couldn't tell how horrified she was. "What…what a lovely surprise."

Beside her, Ty snorted softly. "Good save."

A flashbulb went off nearby and she blinked to clear her vision.

"Keep smiling," Ty warned beneath his breath. "They're reporters."

"Whose idea was this?" she questioned between gritted teeth.

"Your son's."

That changed everything. A more natural smile crept across her mouth and she enveloped Hutch in a hug. "Thank you, sugar."

"You don't mind, do you, Mom?"

She ruffled his pale blond hair. "Of course not," she lied gamely. "What a sweet idea. How in the world did you come up with it?"

"I saw their ad in the newspaper. It's the *Yellow Rose* agency, Mom. Get it? *Yellow roses*. And they use computers."

That explained Hutch's interest—if not what prompted this little venture. "You don't say. Computers, huh? I see why that would appeal. Very scientific."

"You can't lose. Miss Willie's gonna run your application now, and then we'll find out who your date is."

The older woman lifted an eyebrow. "Are you ready?"

Cassidy caught a hint of sympathy in Willie's voice. Apparently, the owner had sensed her lack of enthusiasm. Had she fooled anyone other than Hutch? She slid a quick glance in Ty's direction. Nope. Not likely she'd fool ol' Rumbly Voice. "I'm as ready as I'll ever be," she said with a wry smile.

Willie walked to the computer and punched a series of buttons. A minute later, the laser printer began humming, spitting out an initial page. "Well, my goodness. Will you look at this. It's found a ninety-nine percent match. I don't think I've ever seen that happen on a first try before."

"Who is it?" Hutch demanded. "Is he your best one?"

"A ninety-nine percent match suggests he's an excellent candidate. Can't get much better than that," she confirmed.

Hutch frowned. "I don't know. There's still that bad one percent. Could be a problem."

The next sheet scrolled out of the printer. "Okay. Here come the results. And the winner is…" Her eyes widened in dismay. "Oh, dear."

The reporter and photographer crowded closer, leaning over Willie's shoulder. "What's it say?" The reporter snatched the printout from Willie's hands and frowned. "Ty Merrick. Wait a minute. I know that name…." Like a hound dog tripping over a hot scent, her nose twitched. She pivoted toward Ty, and Cassidy half expected her to start baying as she honed in on her prey. "Hey! That's you."

"Willie! What the *hell* have you done?" Ty snatched

the paper from the reporter's grasp. "This can't be. There must be a mistake."

Cassidy pinched the sheet from between his two fingers to give it a quick look-see. No doubt Ty was right and there'd been an error. These things happened, especially with mechanical oddities like computers. It probably didn't say Ty Merrick at all. No doubt it listed a similar name like Rye Belleck or Sy Serrick or Tom Selleck. Hey! A girl could dream. Or maybe it wasn't her profile they'd run. Sure as shootin'. That's what must have...

She read through the paper three full times before conceding defeat. Texan rancher Ty Merrick was a ninety-nine percent ideal match for waitress Cassidy Lonigan. How that was possible, she couldn't quite figure. But there it sat, topping a full page of bewildering statistics, glaring at her in huge, bold, underscored black print.

Crud.

"There must be a mistake," Ty repeated. "I'm not even in the damn computer."

Willie cleared her throat. "Actually, that's not true. You see, we put you in there as a test case and I guess we forgot to take you out."

"Well, match her with the runner-up."

"There *is* no runner-up. Usually we have three or four close matches. But in this case, there's only one. You."

Hutch grinned. "Happy birthday, Mom. I bought you him." He pointed at Ty. "He's your present."

Oh, joy. "Gosh darn it! That's wonderful. I couldn't be happier." Not bad, she congratulated herself. Got that out without choking or being struck down by lightning. Amazing.

Ty cut through the people separating him from his grandmother and wrapped an arm around her shoulders. "Excuse us for a minute. Willie? We need to talk."

"Can't this wait?" she asked.

Ty regarded her through narrowed eyes. For a woman who never got flustered, his darling grandmother sure as hell looked flustered. "I'm afraid it can't." Cupping her elbow, he marched her across the room. The instant they were out of the reporter's hearing, he demanded, "What the *hell* do you mean, the computer chose me?"

"Now, Ty, don't get your knickers in a knot." Her nervousness had dissipated, replaced with a more typical aggression.

Ty folded his arms across his chest and fixed his grandmother with a cool gaze. "I don't wear knickers, Willie. I never have." The look she returned was every bit as cool as his. A genetic trait, he decided dryly. And an amazing recovery, in view of her earlier agitation. "Now explain how my profile showed up in your computer."

"You were a test case." A thread of defensiveness shot through her voice. "We entered your data when we were first setting up the computer so we could do some trial runs. I thought you'd been deleted."

"But I wasn't."

"No."

"Fine. Delete me now." For the first time in his entire life, he saw Willie blush. It was quite a riveting sight considering her brash personality. Flustered... And now blushing. Something was going on. And come hell or high water, he'd get to the bottom of it. "Willie—"

"I can't delete you," she stated bluntly.

"I'm sure there's a computer expert out there somewhere you can hire to remove the pertinent—"

She waved his remark aside. "It just takes a push of a button."

"Then push it."

"I would except..." She sighed. "Ty, the reporter saw. She knows you're Cassidy's match. I can't delete you now."

"Well, use one of the other names the computer gave you. There's always three or four matches."

"Like I said. Not this time. You were the only one. A ninety-nine percent match at that."

He could practically hear the bone-fracturing sound of a steel-jawed trap snapping closed around him. "Mind explaining how this happened?" he questioned with admirable restraint.

"I can't say. But it did and there isn't anything I can do to change it now." She planted her hands on her hips and stared him down, her clear blue eyes oddly reminiscent of Hutch Lonigan's. "I need you to date this woman."

"And if I say no?"

"That's your choice, of course. I can't force you."

Hah! Why use force when a little grand-maternal guilt would work, as well? "What will happen to the business if I refuse?"

She strove for a stiff-upper-lip sort of look. "Frankly, I'm not sure we could take the adverse publicity, especially after the incident with Wanda."

She didn't pull her punches, and several blistering invectives burned the inside of Ty's mouth, desperate to purple the air. He managed to bite them back. When he'd been a brash, unruly kid, pinched ears and soap mouthwashes had cured him of that youthful indulgence. Now that he was old enough to say what he pleased regardless of the consequences, he had too much respect for the woman who'd raised him to offend her with the salty edge of his tongue. "What would I have to do?"

"Take her out on a few dates."

"How many?"

"As many as it'll take to satisfy her kid."

"That's a tall order, Willie. I don't think he's someone easily satisfied."

His grandmother shrugged. "Maybe she won't like you. Then you'll be off the hook."

He shot her a sharp glance. "But you won't. What happens if she doesn't want me?"

For the first time, a smile slid across Willie's face. "You think that's likely, boy?"

"Anything's possible."

"Right. And maybe the sun will rise in the west and set in the east."

"This isn't going to work, old gal," he said compassionately. "I'm not in the market for someone like Cassidy Lonigan. So either she'll get hurt, the boy'll be hurt or your business will take the hit. I just don't see this ending well, no matter how we handle it."

"There's one possibility you haven't considered."

"What's that?"

She peeped at him from the corner of her eye. "You might actually take a shine to this woman. She might be the one you've been waiting for all these years."

Ty shook his head. "You have a better chance of getting that western sunrise, sweetheart."

"All you have to do is kiss her. Then you'll know for certain."

"Sure, Willie. Whatever you say."

He struggled to ignore the image of wary eyes—large gray eyes that darkened to pewter when outraged and lightened to silver whenever she looked at her son. To ignore the way a halo of hair so dark a brown it bordered on black, surrounded the prettiest face he'd seen in ages. To ignore long, trim arms and legs perfectly made to wrap around a man. What would it be like to kiss Cassidy Lonigan...assuming she didn't kill him in the process? Would her kiss be as sweet as her voice? Or as painful as the back of her hand?

"Will you do it?" his grandmother demanded in an undertone. "Will you take her out?"

There wasn't a single doubt in his mind. He'd do anything for Willie. "I'll date her. But you have to run her profile again and see if there aren't a few alternate candidates you can line up. This kid wants a dad. I'd like to see him get one." He scrutinized Cassidy. "Although I suspect it's going to be one hell of a tough sale."

"Mr. Merrick?" the reporter called. "Could we get a shot of you and Ms. Lonigan?"

"I'd really rather not," Cassidy began.

"We won't print the picture without your permission," the reporter hastened to say. "But we were so intrigued by your son's request, we thought it would make a great story for our readers."

"Don't you like my present?" Hutch piped up, a trace of uncertainty edging his voice. "I bought him just for you."

It was the first hint of vulnerability Ty had ever seen the boy reveal. Striding across the room, he dropped an arm around Cassidy's shoulders and drew her close. "I'm sure your mom is thrilled. She's surprised is all."

Cassidy stiffened within his hold. "Very."

"Relax," he ordered beneath his breath. "The poor kid spent every dime he had for this. You don't want to disappoint him, do you?"

That got through to her. Her eyes widened and he caught a quick glimpse of worried Confederate gray before thick, dark lashes swept downward to conceal her expression. "Thank you, sweetpea. You couldn't have picked a better present."

A flashbulb lit the room again. Then the photographer frowned at them. "How about giving her a kiss?" he suggested. "It would make fantastic copy."

Ty glanced down at Cassidy. Her pink lips were parted in dismay and he suppressed a sudden urge to sample them, to see if they were as sweet as they looked—to see if the honey in her voice flavored her mouth, as well. She went rigid within the circle of his arms. Kissing her probably wasn't a good idea. In fact, if her expression was anything to go by, it was an incredibly bad idea. But for some reason, that tempted him all the more.

"Oh, what the hell," he muttered.

Lowering his head, he captured her tiny gasp of distress. For the space of a heartbeat, his mouth connected with hers in a quick slide of soft, moist lips. He cupped her cheek, determined to taste more of her, to drink in the most delicious sensation he'd ever experienced. Before he could, she jerked free, a hand covering the lower half of her face, stealing from him the promise of paradise.

A growl of annoyance reverberated deep in his chest and he reached for her, prepared to drag her back into his arms. If it hadn't been for the angry defiance flaming to life in her eyes, he'd have done it. He took a deep breath, then another, gathering up his control. What the *hell* had just happened? He'd never lost it like that before. Never forced himself on a woman. Nor had he ever been so affected by a simple—

Kiss.

He sucked air. Damn. Was it possible? Was there something to that ridiculous legend of Willie's? There was only one way to be certain. "We'll definitely have to try that again," he said for her ears alone.

Her annoyance turned to rock-solid determination. "Not a chance."

"We seem to have a match," Willie interrupted with undisguised satisfaction.

"Except for that one percent," Cassidy replied, her full attention focused on Ty. No doubt she'd decided to keep the enemy in sight and at arm's length—all twenty-six inches this time. Smart move. "I'm a bit worried about that."

Ty smiled, outwardly relaxed while inwardly, hunting instincts as old as mankind stirred to life. *Run, sweetheart. Run as fast as you can—while you still can.* It wouldn't stop him, not until they'd shared another kiss. Depending on the result, he'd either let her escape, if that's what she preferred...or bind her tight. "That one percent won't bother me," he warned gently.

"Oh, really?" Her answering smile bit like sugarcoated poison. "What a shame. It bothers the heck out of me."

As Cassidy headed for home on the bus with Hutch, she stared glumly through the dust-grimed window at the bustling San Antonio traffic. Today was sure one for her scrapbook. What in the world was she going to do? Her sweet, wonderful son had played a truly rotten trick. He'd bought her the one thing she wanted least in the world—a man. And he'd done it in a way that prevented her from refusing his little surprise without hurting him. Nor, apparently, could she return the impossible "gift" or trade him in for a different model. Not as long as the computer matched them at ninety-nine percent.

Perhaps it wouldn't have been so bad if Hutch had purchased someone different. Someone safe. Someone she could control. But instead, he'd gone to buy the equivalent of a harmless kitten and come back with a half-starved mountain lion.

Cassidy frowned. Now that she thought about it, that was precisely what Ty reminded her of. The mix of tawny blond and brown strands of hair coupled with those odd green eyes and powerful musculature all added up to one thing. Good ol' Leo the Lion. He even moved with the same sleek assurance, all controlled power and relentless strength. And that kiss!

Her mouth tingled at the memory and she lifted a hand to her lips.

She couldn't remember the last time she'd been kissed. Of course, whenever it'd been, she hadn't panicked like a frightened schoolgirl. Come to think of it, she'd never *been* a frightened schoolgirl. Maybe if she had... Her gaze slid to Hutch. *Don't go there*, she ordered herself. If she'd lived her life differently, she wouldn't have her son. And she loved Hutch with all her heart and soul. Heck, she'd do anything for him.

Cassidy shut her eyes, surrendering to the inevitable. Anything. Including dating a hungry mountain lion.

Ty stood on the porch of Yellow Rose Matchmakers and stared blindly out at the quiet residential street. This wasn't going to be easy. Not even a little. Assuring himself that what he'd shared with Cassidy Lonigan hadn't been a fluke would be a snap compared to what would inevitably follow. It was the next part that would take every ounce of determination and patience he possessed. How did he convince a woman who didn't believe in love that not only did it exist, but that it could be found in a first kiss?

Willie joined him on the porch. "It's happened, hasn't it, boy?"

"I'm not a boy," he retorted mildly.

"You're avoiding the question. Is she the one? Was I right?"

He noticed his grandmother hadn't taken her usual place on the porch swing but stood in the shade, her posture as ramrod straight as always. Only the slight clenching of her arthritic fingers gave away her tension and confirmed his suspicions. "Did the computer really match us?"

"Yes."

"But you knew ahead of time what the results would be." Her silence was all the confirmation he needed and he sighed. "Did you fudge the data, old gal?"

"No."

"Was I really a test case?"

Again there was a long, pregnant pause. "Let's just say Wanda suggested I undelete your profile," she admitted reluctantly.

Ty couldn't help it. He laughed, the sound tinged with irony. "She always was better at matching people than that damned computer."

"Actually, she disagrees with it this time."

He turned and looked at his grandmother, arching his brow in question. "How's that?"

"She says the computer's wrong. It's not a ninety-nine percent match." Willie smiled complacently. "It's a full one hundred percent fer-sure fire perfect fit."

Progress Report
The results aren't quite what I expected. Seems I'm stuck

with The Mountain for my experiment. Don't know if that's going to work out because Mom doesn't like Ty. (He sure likes her, though!) But since I don't have any other choice, I'm going ahead with my plan. I'll see what happens after their first date. If it doesn't go well, I'll have to set Plan B into motion.

CHAPTER THREE

Final Countdown to First Experiment
 Ty called. He promised to stop by today. Something
about Mom's application form. I'm not happy about this
part. I think he's going to have her look it over and
rerun it if it's not right. But if they do that, I may be
dealing with somebody different and... Well, to be hon-
est, I sorta like Ty. I don't think he'd be the type to leave
Mom when the going gets tough. So, if I choose him to
be my dad, I might have to find a way to manipulate the
results if they rerun the form. Perhaps a quick phone
call's in order....

TY SAW Cassidy the instant he stepped into the small café.
She stood beside a table, a huge, overloaded tray in one
hand, a folding stand in the other. With a practiced maneu-
ver, she snapped the stand open and started to lower the
tray onto it. Halfway there, she froze. Her head jerked upward and her gaze swept the room before landing on him.
She'd sensed his presence, he realized with satisfaction.
Good. Her awareness of him was as intense as his for her.

As it turned out, it wasn't good. Her eyes widened, sweet
vulnerability betraying her before she could veil her reaction. The tray wobbled ominously and he caught the subtle
hitch of her breath as a load of plates slid to one side.
Damn. He should have remembered she was a tad on the
uncoordinated side and not surprised her—at least not at
such a critical juncture.

"Cassidy!" His voice cut through the hum of conversation. "Watch it, sweetheart!"

With a gasp, she tried to right the tray, but it was too

late. With almost poetic grace, first one plate, then another somersaulted off her tray. A greasy Tex-Mex burger, fries, a plastic glass brimming with tea and heaps of creamy coleslaw competed with each other to be the first to land on her customer. A particularly aggressive burger won, splatting dead center in his lap. The upper half of the bun spun through the air before lighting on the patty, perching there like a cocked hat.

"Oh, good gravy!" Cassidy dropped the now empty tray onto the stand. She started to reach for the gently steaming burger, then hesitated, apparently thinking better of it. "I'm *so* sorry."

The customer stared in disbelief at his grease-soaked lap for a split second, than leaped to his feet with a yelp of pain. "It's burning!" he shouted, slapping at the front of his trousers. Clumps of food tumbled to the floor, including the offending burger. He glared at her from beneath a cap of dripping coleslaw. "Didn't you hear me? It's burning. Do something!"

Springing into action, Cassidy snatched a pitcher of ice water out of the hands of a nearby waitress and tossed the contents toward the circle of grease. Ice cubes ricocheted off the man from chin to knees.

Ty winced. That had to hurt.

"Is that better?" she asked. "Is it still burning?"

"Better? *Better*!" With an enraged shriek, he erupted from his booth. Tripping over the tray stand, his loafers shot out from under him and he added himself to the debris of dishes and silverware littering the floor.

Shouldn't have worn loafers, Ty decided judiciously, tipping his Stetson to the back of his head. They were ridiculous footwear. Any sane individual would have known that. He folded his arms across his chest and waited to see what further entertainment Cassidy's customer would offer. It wasn't long in coming. The man flailed around on the floor some, making sure his backside was as thoroughly soaked with food and grease as his front side. He also struggled hard to talk. His jaw ground away like he'd bit down on a particularly tough piece of jerky.

"Spit it out," an old-timer encouraged cheerfully from a nearby table.

The man flopped around some more, his face turning an interesting shade of purplish red. Finally, his voice kicked in, blasting out at full volume. "I'm going to *kill* you, you stupid…"

Oops. Entertainment over. Ty didn't wait to hear any more.

While the man tossed dishes aside in an attempt to regain his footing, Ty loped over to Cassidy. Sweeping her safely behind him, he leaned down and hauled the man to his feet. "Easy does it, friend. It was an accident. The lady apologized, so I suggest you let it go."

"Get the hell out of my way, *friend*. My beef is with her, not you."

The customer kicked a plate out of his way, sending it smashing into a nearby chair. His petty act caused his heel to slip on a lemon wedge and sent him tumbling to the floor again. Ty shook his head. Dumb move. Real dumb— not to mention messy. Any puddles of food the fella had missed last time, he took the opportunity to visit on this occasion. Of course, the man's nasal accent betrayed him as being from one of those states decidedly north of the Mason-Dixon line and well east of the Mississippi. Quite likely that explained his less-than-gentlemanly behavior. The poor Yank had grown up disadvantaged.

"Your beef isn't with the lady any longer," Ty explained gently. "Now it's with me." Cassidy stirred against his back and he knew she was going to do something incredibly foolish—like interfere.

Sure enough, she tugged on his shirt. "This isn't your concern, Ty. I can handle it. I have experience with this sort of thing."

He stifled a groan. Of course she had. No doubt legions of customers had been on the receiving end of her special brand of service. If they'd been anywhere else, he'd have laughed at the absurdity. As it was, he didn't dare take his gaze off the irate customer. "You're not helping any, sweetheart. If you'd just let me—"

She tugged at his shirt some more, putting a severe strain on the seams. An ominous popping sound came from the threads in the vicinity of his shoulders. "Please, Ty!" The soft way she continued to pronounce his name tied his guts in a knot, destroying his focus. "You're going to lose me my job."

"I don't think you need my help with that," he advised after due consideration. "You seemed to be accomplishing that quite well on your own."

"How can you say such a thing?" She yanked at his poor, abused shirt again, snapping a few more vital threads.

"Perhaps it has something to do with him." Ty jerked his thumb toward her former customer who'd just managed to slip-slide to his feet.

"Move aside," the man unwisely ordered. "I have a small matter to discuss with that little bit—"

Ty cut him off before he could finish spitting out the word. "Watch your mouth, son, or I might have to watch it for you," he warned, crushing his Stetson more firmly on his head. It wouldn't do for it to hit the floor should a scuffle ensue—not considering the tile's current condition.

"What did he call me?" Cassidy interjected, outraged. Her arm forgot it was twenty-six inches and clipped Ty's left ear. She shook her finger in the general direction of her customer. "You watch your mouth, mister."

"I believe I just said that," Ty thought to mention.

Her arm shot past his ear again. This time, he was quick enough to duck. The finger got another thorough workout as she continued scolding. "There are ladies and children present, in case you hadn't noticed."

And every one of them was watching with openmouthed fascination.

"So? I don't give a sh—" Ty carefully gathered up the

man's collar, cutting off the flow of air to his lungs. Whatever the man had been about to say ended in a high-pitched squeak.

"Now then," Ty said, taking charge. Or at least trying to. "Let me explain a few things to you, friend. What happened was a real shame. And as much as it rankles for me to admit it, Cassidy does have a small organizational problem with her arms and legs." He loosened his grip on the man's collar a tad. The poor fella was looking a bit blue around the gills. "But if you try to hurt this woman or offend these customers with more unmannerly language, I'll be forced to do something about it."

For the first time, the man seemed to notice the size of the obstacle between him and his goal. He sucked air into his lungs. "Like what?" he asked a trifle less belligerently.

Ty removed one callused hand from the man's collar and held it up for inspection. He'd always considered his hands absurdly large. Evidently, the customer thought so, too. Ty folded his fingers into a ham-size fist. "Does this answer your question?"

"Ty?" Cassidy tried to peek around his shoulders. Fortunately, they were bulky enough to make that a near impossible feat. A few more shirt threads split. By the sudden loosening of his right sleeve, he suspected she'd eliminated at least one seam. "What are you doing? I can't see."

"I'm just being neighborly."

Bewilderment edged her honeyed voice. "Neighborly?"

It was hard to maintain an intimidating facade with a sleeve drooping around one wrist, swallowing the fist he might need to plant on her customer's nose. But he persevered. "I'm explaining to our newfound friend that he was trespassing on private property. He's agreed not to do it again." He gave the customer a gentle shake to encourage his cooperation. "Right?"

The man gawked at Ty's exposed biceps and swallowed. "Yeah. Yeah, right."

"What private property?" Cassidy piped up. "Whatever are you talking about?"

A few of the surrounding customers chuckled. One was even stupid enough to clue her in by waving a clenched fist in the air. Damn.

"You didn't threaten him?" she demanded in outrage. His back received the punishing impact of an elbow, a thumping index finger and possibly her knee. It was hard to tell. Maybe he should have left this guy to her mercy after all. Probably would have served him right. "Ty, you have to leave. Now. Go wait in your car and I'll be with you in a few minutes."

Nothing like having his authority undercut. He felt all of five years old. "I can't do that, Cassidy. The only thing between you and certain death is me," he explained patiently.

"I'm sure you're exaggerating."

Ty contemplated her customer's hopeful expression. "I'm equally sure I'm not."

The owner chose that moment to approach from wherever he'd been hiding. "What's going on here? What's happened?" he questioned as though he hadn't seen a blessed thing.

The customer gestured toward Ty and Cassidy, a malicious light entering his now less-than-intimidated gaze. "Your waitress dumped her tray on me. She's ruined my clothes. And she probably caused a severe burn to my...to my..."

"Peter, Paul and Mary?" Ty offered helpfully.

"Never mind where! I'm going to the doctor right away. You'll have my bill in the morning. If she's still here when I come again..." He started to point at Cassidy, ran up against Ty's chest and thought better of it. "I'm going to sue!"

"Totally unnecessary," the owner said. "Cassidy? I'm sorry, dear. But you're fired."

"*Again*? Gosh darn it, Freddie. How long this time?"

Her boss slid a quick glance at his irate customer. "Permanently, I'm afraid. I won't dock your wages for the cost of the dishes or this gentleman's expenses, but it might be best if you left now."

Ty wrapped an arm around her shoulders. "Come on, sweetheart. You don't need this sort of hassle."

"No, I don't. But I *do* need to eat and pay my rent," she argued. "Come on, Freddie. Be a darlin'. I can't afford to lose my job. How about if I went back to washing up?"

Her boss shuddered. "You about bankrupted me with all the dishes you broke. That's why I made you a waitress."

"I could bus tables."

"Please, Cassidy. Don't say stuff like that. You know I'm on heart medication. Look…I'll provide you with a good recommendation. Heck, I'll even lie." Freddie shrugged. "Best I can do, under the circumstances."

"There's not a chance you're going to save this job," Ty informed her in an undertone. "The best thing you can do is walk away. I'll help you find another one. With the Fiesta coming up, it shouldn't be too tough." At least, not until she'd worked her new job for a few hours and her employer saw her in action. "If push comes to shove, I'll hire you myself." He'd have to find a nice, safe occupation for her—like stuffing pillows or something.

"But—"

"Please, Cassidy," Freddie whispered, "I can't afford the trouble."

That stopped her. With a dignity that impressed the hell out of Ty, she whipped off her apron and handed it to the owner. "I'll be back tomorrow for my paycheck. Thanks for hiring me in the first place."

Without another word, she headed for the exit, words of encouragement following her the entire way. Clearly, she was well liked here. Ty grimaced. With one annoying exception. It was a darned shame.

She turned on him the instant they hit the sidewalk in

front of the café. "Do you have any idea what you've done?" she demanded.

"Saved your hide?"

"You got me fired!"

He corralled her toward his pickup. "The way I see it, I saved you from a customer bent on rearranging that pretty face of yours."

"I—you..." He'd actually managed to distract her. Amazing. "You think I'm pretty?"

A smile tugged at the corner of his mouth. Drop-dead gorgeous would be more accurate. Hadn't anyone told her that before? At a guess...no. Well, that would change. Right now. "I think you're beautiful."

Rose-soft color highlighted her sweeping cheekbones. "Why...thanks. But that still doesn't let you off the hook." She worked on rekindling her anger with a regrettable amount of success. So she wasn't one to have her head turned with flattery, he noted. Good for her. "I needed that job. If you'd have just let me handle it—"

"You'd have been a shade wiser and a hell of a lot sorer."

She hesitated, her vulnerability peeking out again, turning her eyes to charcoal. "Do you really think he'd have hurt me?"

"If he'd ever gotten his footing, he'd have decked you." While she chewed that over, he opened the door to his pickup and loaded her in. With any luck, by the time she awoke to her surroundings, they'd be under way. "I'm sorry I lost you that job. I'll put out a couple of feelers tomorrow."

"No, thanks," came her immediate response. "I can manage on my own."

"I'm sure you could," he agreed, stripping off his ruined shirt. He reached into the back seat of the extended cab and grabbed the spare tee he kept there. He couldn't help but notice that her eyes tried to swallow up her face and her mouth went fishing for flies. Apparently, there was something about him she liked. She turned her head away so fast her braid did the Texas two-step and he buried a grin. *Too late, sweetheart. I already caught you staring.* He climbed behind the wheel and started the engine. "You'll let me help you find a job anyway."

"Why's that?" she questioned, a hint of strain threading her voice.

"Because, as you pointed out, I was partially responsible for getting you fired." He pulled into traffic, pleased that she hadn't insisted he off-load her at the nearest bus stop. Seeing him bare-chested must have thrown her good and proper. He'd have to remember that. "This way, I have a chance to redeem myself."

"Oh. Okay, then. You can help."

He half expected her agreement to sound grudging. It didn't. It came across as... Generous. As though *she* was helping *him*. The sheer illogic of it amused him no end. She didn't want his assistance finding a job because it ran counter to her independent nature. But if her compliance would make him feel better, she was happy to go along. Crazy woman. He slid her a quick look. Crazy, kissable woman.

"You never did say what you were doing at the café," she prompted, the beginning of a frown puckering her brow.

"I came to talk to you about the Yellow Rose." That much was true enough. He wouldn't mention his other reason. With luck, he'd just *do* it, assuming the opportunity presented itself.

Her frown deepened. "I was afraid of that."

"I know you're not happy about these dates, so I thought we'd go over your application privately and rerun it. That way, we can make sure you're matched with the best possible candidate."

"I don't want to date anyone."

"I understand that. But for Hutch's sake, you're going to have to. I figured you should at least have a decent selection of men." Damned magnanimous of him, all things considered. Not that Cassidy saw it that way.

She set her chin in a manner identical to Hutch. So that's where the little squirt had learned it. "I don't want even one man, let alone a whole slew of them."

"I wasn't exactly offering a slew," he retorted, vaguely insulted. "Just a couple of alternatives."

With a little sigh, she leaned back against the seat. Her careworn hands bunched the skirt of her dress, pleating the light blue folds before smoothing out the creases. "Hutch thinks he's being helpful."

"I know." He waited.

"I'm...I'm not interested in a relationship."

"I know that, too."

"So why are you doing this? Why agree to date me?"

For a brief instant, he was tempted to explain about the kiss. Considering how skittish she was about this dating business, he thought better of it. Instead, he decided to show her. He pulled the pickup to the curb outside her apartment complex and switched off the engine.

Unbuckling his seat belt, he leaned across the space separating them and unfastened hers, as well. "What happened last time made me curious."

She stilled, freezing up so fast it felt like a blue norther had lost its way and come screaming down on San Antonio, bringing with it a blast of icy arctic air. "What are you talking about?" She knew. Knew, but refused to admit it aloud.

"I'm talking about that kiss."

Her misty gray eyes widened in alarm. But he caught the momentary glimmer of another reaction, as well. A hint of answering curiosity. "Nothing happened," she protested. "We barely even touched lips."

Ever so cautiously, he cradled her face in his palms. Her skin was soft. So soft he worried about scraping her with the roughness of his hands. "Then there's nothing to be concerned about."

"I'm not," she fibbed.

The lie was so blatantly transparent, he didn't bother calling her on it. "Good. So this time when I kiss you, you won't get angry, right?"

While she took a few precious seconds to weigh the pros and cons of her response to that one, he eased her deeper into his embrace. She didn't resist, didn't protest, so he did what came naturally. He kissed her. Fully. Like he'd wanted to ever since that last aborted encounter. Their lips met as though they'd practiced a thousand times before. Joined easily, melded completely. She tasted incredible, like a brand new flavor he sensed would be his permanent favorite.

His reaction was as instantaneous as last time and far more intense—perhaps because it was a real kiss rather than a fleeting touch of lips. So much for needing further proof. *One kiss and he'd know.* And he did. Knew with every fiber of his being. Cassidy Lonigan was his future—a sweet, hot, delicious, permanent sort of future.

He didn't rush. The woman in his arms wasn't a treat he intended to hurry. Hell, she wasn't a treat at all. More like…destiny. And one didn't fight destiny any more than one galloped headlong through it. One worked toward it, fulfilled it, explored it. And enjoyed the hell out of it. He sank into her, intensifying the kiss. Yeah. One enjoyed every destined moment.

She made a small sound deep in her throat, an intriguing combination of surrender and rebellion. Her hands flattened on his shoulders even as her tongue crept into his mouth, slipping home like a thief in the night. It surprised him. He'd never thought Cassidy a woman of half measures. She struck him as the all-or-nothing type. And she proved it the next instant.

Rolling onto one hip, she wrapped her arms in a stranglehold around his neck and slanted her mouth more fully over his. And then she consumed him as if he was an ice-cold dessert served up on a scorching hot afternoon. She wriggled closer and her knee plowed onto his lap, damn near emasculating him. Sheer instinct had him catching her leg just in the nick of time, his palm rasping across her bare skin.

Her gasp burst into his mouth and he absorbed the slight shudder that shot through her. Curious to confirm the cause, he stroked his hand upward from her knee. Her pulse jolted in response and a soft moan of longing reverberated against his chest. How long had it been since she'd last been touched, he wondered, since a man had slipped a hand beneath her dress and given her pleasure? Had anyone ever caressed the sensitive skin along her thighs or massaged the taut muscles of her legs until she relaxed so deeply she couldn't move? Did anyone ever see to her needs, or was she the one who always gave? It struck him as past time that she be on the receiving end of a little TLC.

She broke off the kiss with a groan and buried her face in the crook of his neck. "I'm so sorry. I can't believe I did that."

"Nothing to apologize for. I'm sure as hell not offended," he soothed with a tender smile. "But next time, I think we'll pick someplace a little more private."

Cassidy peered around in surprise, as though just realizing their location. Her eyes grew wide again. "How do you know where I live?"

"Hutch supplied your address when he filled out the application."

"Oh." She didn't look pleased. "You mean we've been sitting outside my apartment—"

"Necking," he offered helpfully.

"I can't believe this happened." She ripped free of his arms and glared at him. "This is all your fault."

"You're right. And I take full responsibility for your forcing yourself on me." He nudged the conversation in a slightly different direction before she gathered her wits enough to verbalize her indignation. "Can you arrange for someone to stay with Hutch for the next few hours while

we review your application? I thought we could go somewhere private and decide how to handle it. Maybe have
dinner together.''

"After what just happened?"

He wasn't quite certain what one had to do with the
other. But she'd seen a connection, which was the important part. "All the more reason, don't you think?"

She stewed for a moment. "I—I don't know. I guess we
could.''

If that was an agreement, it was one of the most reluctant
he'd ever heard. "Is that a yes?" he asked.

She hesitated for a split second more, then nodded. "It's
a yes. We might as well get it over with.''

"Gee, thanks.''

She had the grace to blush, not that she retracted anything. Stubborn woman. "I was scheduled to work tonight
anyway," she said. "So I've already arranged for a neighbor to keep an eye on Hutch. If you'd give me a minute to
change, I'd appreciate it.''

"Sure thing.''

He'd hoped she'd ask him up to her apartment. He didn't
want to push, but the more he learned about her, the more
comfortable he'd feel about that kiss they'd shared. He still
had a tough time believing she was the woman he'd spend
the rest of his life with. Two days ago, he'd have sworn
that people couldn't fall in love at first kiss—until he'd
locked lips with Cassidy.

"Care to invite me up?" he prompted, well aware she
had no intention of doing any such thing.

"I wasn't planning to," she confirmed with devastating
honesty.

"I realize that." He gestured toward the apartment building. "But since Hutch has his nose pressed to the window,
you might want to change your plans.''

"There's not much to see," she informed him casually.
Too casually.

He reached out and tugged on the end of her French

braid, wondering why she didn't want him to join her. It was almost as though she had something to hide. "It's going to happen at some point. You might as well get it over with."

Her breath escaped in a gusty sigh. "I'm being ungracious, aren't I? My Aunt Esther always told me it was one of the worst sins I could commit."

"Oh, I'd have thought there were a few worse ones."

"You're right," Cassidy confessed. "And I even came up with one or two of them to prove it." She offered a charmingly crooked smile. "Okay. I'll be polite. Would you care to come in for a cup of coffee, Mr. Merrick?"

He inclined his head. "Thank you, Ms. Lonigan. I'd like that very much."

It didn't take long to troop up the two flights of stairs to her front door. Hutch stood there waiting for them. "Hiya, Ty."

"Hey there, kid." He started to ruffle the thatch of blond hair, but at the last instant thought better of it. No doubt Hutch considered himself too old for that. Instead, Ty fisted his hand and held it out, carefully bumping knuckles with the boy. It wouldn't do to accidently bruise him. He suspected Cassidy wouldn't take it well.

"Mrs. Welch just left," Hutch said as they walked inside the apartment. "We're supposed to let her know if you want me to stay with her this evening. So..." He cocked his head to one side. "What are you doing home?"

"I..." A blush licked at her cheekbones as she closed the door. "I was fired."

Hutch's mouth dropped open. "*Again*? What happened this time?"

She darted a quick glance in Ty's direction, then looked hastily away. "I was distracted and dropped a tray on a customer," she muttered.

Hutch whistled. "Wow. That's a new one."

She scowled at Ty, letting him know where she placed

the blame for the incident. "With any luck, it won't happen again."

"Man, I'd be really ticked if someone dropped a tray on me. Was he hurt? Did he yell? Did he kick up a ruckus? Is that why you got fired?"

She suffered her son's questions with amazing good humor. "Fortunately, Ty kept the customer from getting too upset."

Hutch stilled. "Ty was there, huh? When you dropped the tray?" A knowing gleam sparked in his bright blue eyes. Damn, but the kid was smart. "*Int*eresting."

Cassidy's color deepened, raging across her face like an out-of-control brushfire. "Yes, he was there. Now, if you don't mind, I have to change. Mr. Merrick and I are going…are going…" She trailed off in confusion.

"On your first date?" Hutch offered helpfully.

"I guess you could call it that," she admitted. *If it gets one of their dates out of the way*, Ty read between the lines. "We're going to review my application form. Why don't you entertain Mr. Merrick while I get ready. See if he'd like a drink."

"Okay."

Head held high, Cassidy swept from view, the door to her bedroom shutting behind her just shy of a slam. Through the hollow-core panel, Ty heard an odd scuffling noise and Cassidy's muffled voice saying something he couldn't quite catch. But before he could ask about it, Hutch spoke up.

"She's never done that before, you know," he commented.

"Slammed the door?"

"No. Dropped a tray on somebody."

"I'm relieved to hear it. Though I suppose it was only a matter of time."

Hutch snickered. "She does trip a lot. She keeps saying it's because she's shorter in her head than in real life."

Ty grinned ruefully. "Trust me. I know all about those extra three inches."

"Yeah." Hutch matched his grin—a purely masculine moment. "They sometimes get me, too. Especially when she gets excited and starts waving her arms around. Gotta be a fast ducker. You wanna sit?"

Ty eyed the two ancient chairs the living area had to offer. A scrapbook stuffed with papers rested on one. He could just read what had been scrawled across one of the loose bits of paper: *Great new apartment. Very roomy.* He glanced around. She considered this roomy? His closet had more space. He examined the chair again. It probably couldn't handle much more weight than the scrapbook, he decided. The other wasn't much better. Neither looked capable of containing him for longer than two seconds flat before splintering. "I'll stand, thanks."

"Okay. You wanna drink?"

"Sure."

He followed Hutch into the kitchen. There wasn't much furniture in here, either, though the place had been scrubbed spotless, as if to make up for the vast expanse of emptiness. A table had been pushed against the far wall, one leg shored up with a phone book. Two mismatched chairs were tucked neatly underneath each end. Squashed next to the counter was a refrigerator older than Willie. As far as he could see, they didn't own any small appliances—no toaster or coffeemaker, let alone a microwave.

Hutch rummaged in one of the cupboards and Ty caught a glimpse of the contents. Two plates, two bowls and two glasses. That was it. It told a grim story. The boy removed one of the glasses, opened a nearly empty refrigerator and grabbed a quart of milk. He poured Ty a glass and handed it to him.

"I didn't think the computer was gonna pick you," the kid commented as he returned the carton to the refrigerator.

Ty took a swallow of milk, guilt souring the taste. It wasn't bad enough he'd helped Cassidy out of a job. Now he was as good as snatching the last drop of milk from their mouths. *You don't need this sort of hassle*, he'd blithely told her. *The best thing you can do is walk away.* Hah! Did she have any financial reserves to get by on until she found another job? He suddenly realized that Hutch was waiting for an answer and shrugged. "I didn't know the computer would pick me, either. But I'm glad it did."

"You like my mom?"

"Yes." He forced himself to finish the milk and wondered if there was any tactful way of restocking her fridge. Knowing Cassidy and her independent streak, he rather doubted it.

"You want to marry her?" Hutch asked, catching Ty off guard.

Damn, the kid was direct. "It's a bit early to tell, don't you think?"

Hutch didn't reply. He simply waited.

Aw, hell. If it hadn't been for that damned kiss... "I'm giving it serious consideration."

The chin jutted out an inch. "I'm part of the package, too, you know."

"I knew that going in," Ty reassured him gently.

Gradually, Hutch relaxed. "Okay. Do you want to see my room?"

"Sure." Carefully washing the empty glass, Ty upended it on the drain board.

Hutch's room proved to be a revelation. Shoved in one corner was a mattress, minus a box spring or frame. Instead of a dresser, cartons lined one wall, with clothes neatly folded in each. The rest of the room was dominated by a huge desk—and a very expensive state-of-the-art computer. That simple fact told him more clearly than anything else where Cassidy's priorities lay.

"Nice setup."

Hutch glanced uncertainly at him. "The school told her to get me one. I'm..." He snatched a quick breath and then said in a rush, "You better know right off. I'm smart."

Ty nodded. "I figured as much."

"No. I mean I'm *really* smart," Hutch emphasized. "Scary smart. So if that's gonna bother you, maybe you should say so now before…" Resolutely, he turned his face toward the computer. "Before anybody gets their feelings hurt."

"Hutch." The boy ignored him, busying himself with the machine. "Look at me, please."

Reluctantly, Hutch lifted his gaze to Ty's. Settling his glasses more firmly on the bridge of his upturned nose, he braced himself. "Yeah?"

"It doesn't bother me."

"Okay."

"Look at me and listen to what I'm saying to you, kid." Brilliant blue eyes fastened on Ty's face again, a desperate kind of hope burning in the apprehensive gaze. "Smart's okay with me. Even scary smart. I don't have a problem with it and I won't. Got that?"

The chin wobbled. "Yeah. I got it."

"Good. Now, why don't you show me how this thing works."

The next few minutes passed with Hutch chattering away a mile a minute. Ty could see why the school had recommended a computer for the boy. Did they have any idea, though, what a financial sacrifice it had been? He doubted it. He suspected Cassidy Lonigan's pride came in as abundant a helping as her generosity.

"Hutch? Where…?" She appeared in the doorway then and smiled uncertainly. "Oh. There you two are. Everything all right?"

"Great! Ty knows almost as much about computers as I do."

She lifted her eyebrows, impressed. "Wow. That's quite a compliment."

She'd brushed out her braid so her hair fell in a straight dark curtain to cup her shoulders. She'd also changed from her uniform into a light gray, short-sleeved blouse and matching slacks. Looked like he wouldn't be slipping his hand under her skirt again today, Ty realized regretfully. A damn shame.

"You look great," he said. And she did. Fantastic, in fact, despite the lack of a skirt. The slacks emphasized her endless legs and narrow hips, while the soft color made her eyes more intense than usual. "Ready to go?"

"I guess."

Her enthusiasm underwhelmed him, but he simply grinned. "Good."

She avoided his gaze, fixing her attention on her son. "I'll call you from the restaurant and give you the phone number. And I'll send Mrs. Welch over, although I think she wants to watch you at her place tonight."

"Okay."

She dropped a kiss on the top of his head. "Don't open the door without looking to see who it is."

Hutch glanced at Ty and grimaced. *Women*, his expression said. "I know."

Still she hovered and Ty suspected that if she wasn't wringing her hands, he and Hutch would be doing some fast maneuvering to get clear of those twenty-six inches. "I won't be late."

"Have fun and goodbye," Hutch said meaningfully.

She'd run out of things to say and knew it. Surrendering to the inevitable, she walked to the door. Turning, she announced, "I'll see you *soon*." Apparently, that pointed declaration satisfied her, for she allowed Ty to tow her from the apartment without too much of a struggle.

The instant they left, Hutch frowned. Part of his plan was working. The computer had picked the perfect man for a father. But his mom was proving to be a bit of a problem. Calling up a certain file, he keyed in his password to open it and began typing.

Progress Report

Bad news. Mom hasn't changed her mind about Ty even though they kissed. They don't know I saw, but I did. Course, his losing her job for her didn't help. You'd think he'd have thought of that! For sure that smacker he planted on her should have made her want him for a husband. But, noooo!

Conclusion

Maybe those things take time. Maybe you have to be exposed to a bunch of kisses before they take effect, like germs or something. She hasn't caught a love cold yet, cuz they haven't been around each other long enough. Or maybe he's catchier than she is. If that's the case, we'll have to be where he can infect her more often.

Proposed Response

I talked to Miss Willie about the changes Ty's gonna make to the application form and she promised to make sure it didn't reject him. So I have that front covered. As for further infecting Mom... Looks like Plan B will have to be put in motion after all.

Finished, Hutch printed up his latest entries, folded the pages carefully and slipped them into a preaddressed envelope. Tomorrow he'd mail it.

Just as he'd promised.

CHAPTER FOUR

Experiment #1: Protective Instincts
*Goal: To bring out the protective instincts in Ty.
According to the documentary I watched at school last
month, the male in the animal kingdom will protect his
mate from harm. So let's see whether or not he's capable
of that. Because if he's not, he isn't the right man for
Mom.*
*Procedure: I hate to do this to my own mother, but she's
gonna have a bit of bad luck....*

"SO, WHERE are we going?" Cassidy demanded the instant
they left her apartment building.

She probably should have asked instead of demanded.
Aunt Esther had done her best to drum graciousness and
tact into Cassidy's stubborn psyche. Unfortunately for all
concerned, the lessons hadn't taken.

She shot Ty a disgruntled look. He'd had the upper hand
in what passed as their relationship for far too long and
she'd had a *really* bad day, thanks to him. Asserting herself
would clue him in to that fact. At least, that was the plan.
"Well?" she prompted impatiently.

To her frustration, he waited until they were both settled
in his oversize truck again and buckled into their seat
belts before replying. "We're going someplace private.
Someplace where we can get to know each other and talk
without interruption."

No wonder he'd trapped her in his pickup before answering. A knot formed in the pit of her stomach—or was
it a hangman's noose that threatened to choke her? Maybe
both. "How private?" This time she asked. Nicely.

"Very."

"Like a private restaurant, right?"

"Not exactly."

Uh-oh. Panic set in. He was a man; she was a woman. He'd kissed her. She'd dissolved into a pathetic puddle. And now it was vital she find the means to slip away before he touched her again and started the process all over. "I'll need to let Hutch know where I am," she babbled. "He has to be able to reach me in case there's a problem. I can't just—"

"Easy, sweetheart. Relax. My jacket's on the back seat. There's a phone in the pocket. Call Hutch and I'll give him my private number. That way, he can reach us no matter where we are." He glanced at her, his green eyes calm yet implacable. "On this, or any of our future dates."

Her alarm intensified. "You're assuming there's going to be more than one."

"It isn't an assumption." He braked for a red light and turned to look at her, resting his arms along the top of the steering wheel. He filled his side of the truck, his shoulders impossibly broad, the power of his arms straining the fabric of his shirt. "It's a fact."

"Stop doing that," she groused. "It's not fair."

He lifted a tawny brow. "Doing what?"

"Looking like…" Gesturing toward all the deliciously male parts that kept distracting her every time he flexed, she accidently clipped his shoulder. To her relief, he hardly flinched at all. "*That.* It doesn't give me a fair chance when we argue."

For a brief instant, something hot and primitive flared to life in his gaze. If the light hadn't turned green then, she knew he would have kissed her. Again. "All *that* bothers you?"

Would she ever learn to keep her mouth shut? "Only when you tense it up so the ripply stuff shows through your clothes," she muttered.

"And if I wasn't wearing any clothes?"

So she'd actually *see* the ripples in all their naked glory, like when he'd changed his shirt earlier? No way would she answer that one! She might think about it for a spell or two or drool a bit, but he wouldn't drag a single blessed word out of her on the subject.

Her silence must have blabbed because his chuckle rumbled over to her side of the pickup and eased into her pores. She could feel an ache building—an ache for something she'd spent years burying beneath a hard-won control. Did he know what that laugh did to her? He must. Somehow he'd discovered how long it had been since she'd last been with a man and— He interrupted before she could finish her thought, thank heaven.

"Next time we argue, I'll strip down to guarantee an easy win."

Cassidy stifled a groan at the image. Why couldn't he be sensible? More importantly, why couldn't she? "If you'd just do things my way, that wouldn't be necessary," she explained.

His dark voice reached for her again, wrapping her in warmth. "Do you really think that's going to happen?"

No. "Absolutely."

To her intense relief, he didn't laugh outright. "Face it, sweetheart. You're stuck with me. Your son purchased the San Antonio Fiesta Special from Yellow Rose Matchmakers. That means you date me or one of the other candidates the computer picks until the Fiesta's over. Since the computer only coughed up one match so far, it looks like I'm all yours for the next month."

Did that also mean she was all his? Oh, no. Not a chance. "Hutch couldn't possibly have had the money for something like that," Cassidy protested.

Ty grinned. "Willie gave him a bargain. You'll be pleased to know that I came at the rock bottom price of nine dollars plus change. He'd have made it ten, but he needed bus fare to get back home."

Her pride did a quick jump start and she struggled to

keep it under control—without notable success. "How much does it really cost?"

"That's not important."

"It is to me. If he didn't pay enough—"

"Don't bother finishing the thought. There's no point."

"I can't take advantage of your grandmother's generosity. It wouldn't be right. Besides, I don't like being obligated."

"Too bad. It would offend her if you refused the discount. The deal she made was with the boy, not you. And since she runs the Yellow Rose, she's allowed to strike any deal she wants."

Cassidy gave up. She wasn't going to win this particular fight and she knew it. She slid Ty an assessing glance. Considering his earlier threat, if she pushed, he'd start whipping off his clothing. And as interesting a sight as that would be, surrendering to his stronger will seemed the best option for her mental health. For now, at any rate. "Thank you. That's very kind of Miss Willie."

"See? That didn't choke you too badly."

A smile teased her lips. "It darn near killed me," she retorted.

"Hardly showed at all."

She settled against the bench seat and forced herself to relax. "So where are we going that's so private?"

"My place."

She jerked back upright. Crud. "I don't think—"

Ty released a sigh of exasperation. "Do you argue over everything?"

"Just about," she answered with painful honesty. "But I have a point this time. It's not appropriate to go to a man's place on the first date." Good grief. If she didn't know better, she'd have sworn she'd opened her mouth and Aunt Esther had voiced one of her "rules".

"Old-fashioned girl, huh?"

"Not really. Let's just say I learned common sense the hard way." Maybe the hardest way possible.

"I'll behave." He gave her another of those cool green glances—the sort that warned he was always in control and she'd do well to remember it. "Willie'd have my hide if I didn't."

"Hah." Cassidy folded her arms across her chest. "Don't tell me she could slow you down once you'd made up your mind about something."

"She's been known to put a damper on my enthusiasm from time to time."

"But she hasn't stopped you," Cassidy guessed shrewdly.

"Not when I want something bad enough."

She doubted he meant it as a warning. Still, she intended to take it that way. The sensation of being hunted returned full bore. Ty exuded an innate patience and determination that matched the sheer size and power of the man. Instinct told her that once he'd fixed his sights on a quarry, he'd track it relentlessly. Capturing his prey would only be a matter of time, his success a given. More and more she'd begun to suspect he'd fixed his sights on her. Whether he'd done it at the request of his grandmother or to help Hutch, she couldn't guess. But unless she found a way to dissuade him, he'd have her in the end—something she preferred to avoid at all costs.

For the hour it took to reach his place, she worried endlessly about how to extricate herself from her latest predicament. Finally, she gave it up as pointless. Why fuss about what she couldn't fix? She'd had that particular lesson drummed into her more than once. Too bad she was such a slow learner. Ty turned into a gated entranceway just then, which succeeded in distracting her. As they bumped along the gravel road, she focused on their destination—a large homestead that topped a bluff and overlooked an endless spread of cattle country.

"Is all this yours?" she asked in astonishment.

"Yes."

She studied the impressive building as they approached.

The main part of the house had been roughly hewn from logs, with succeeding generations expanding from there, combining wood with stone as the house sprawled outward from its well-aged core. "It looks old. Has your family owned it for long?"

"It's been in Merrick hands for a while now."

"How long's a while?"

He shrugged. "Think Alamo and add a handful of years."

"Your roots go deep."

She couldn't help voicing the wistful observation. What would it be like to have the land of your forebears beneath your feet? To know that generation after generation had lived and died, loved and cried, laughed and grieved on the same spot. She'd give almost anything to be connected to that long a lineage, to help continue it.

To belong.

Yearning turned to determination. Okay. So she didn't have a heritage to match Ty's, nor could she offer one to Hutch. That didn't mean she couldn't make a home for them. As soon as she'd saved enough, they'd have their own house. It might not be like this, but it would be a start. She'd learned long ago that thirsty roots dug deep. Soon she'd belong somewhere, too.

"What's wrong?"

She'd been so preoccupied with her thoughts and plans, she hadn't realized they'd stopped. Ty's all too observant gaze was fixed on her face. How much had she given away? she wondered uneasily.

"I was thinking about what it must be like to have a family history like yours." She waved a hand toward his home. "A connection to the past."

"Proud. Comfortable. And frustrating," he answered promptly.

"Frustrating?" She swiveled to look at him. "Why?"

"It comes with a lot of responsibility."

Her eyes narrowed. "You have a problem with that?"

"No. But my father did. He felt trapped by his legacy."

"Did he run?" The question escaped before she'd considered the wisdom of asking it.

"Yes." It was his turn to level a narrowed gaze on her. "Familiar with that response, are you?"

Cassidy escaped the car as though sprung from a trap, nearly hanging herself before she remembered to unclasp her seat belt. Ty exited, as well, only he did it without incident. He reached into the back seat of the extended cab and recovered the cell phone from his jacket.

"Why don't we get this over with?" she suggested uncomfortably, as he dropped the compact phone into the pocket of his jeans. Anything to end their conversation.

"I assume you mean our first date."

She had the grace to blush at his dry tone. "I'm sorry. I didn't..." Setting her jaw, she turned to confront him over the width of the truck's hood. "Actually, that's precisely what I meant. I apologize for being rude about it. But to be honest, I'm not interested in dating anyone."

"You haven't told Hutch you feel that way."

She shrugged. "It hasn't come up."

"Hutch isn't waiting for your ex to sweep back into your lives?"

"No."

"Then I gather I won't have to worry about that, either." There was no mistaking his satisfaction.

Cassidy studied the taut planes and angles of Ty's tanned face, wishing she could read his expression as easily as she used to read her ex-husband's. Unfortunately, Ty was more self-contained, which unnerved her no end. The need to escape intensified, growing in direct proportion to the aggressive gleam in his eyes.

She tumbled into speech. "You're doing this for your grandmother's sake, right? I know from what you said at the Yellow Rose that you weren't supposed to be in the computer. It was all an...an accident. These dates...they're just for show. Aren't they?"

He circled the pickup, his movements slow and measured and deliberate. Even so simple an act spoke of tightly caged power. "Yes, I agreed to date you for my grandmother's sake. No, I wasn't supposed to be in the computer. As to whether or not it was all an accident, only my grandmother and Wanda know the answer to that." He stopped directly in front of her. "And finally, if imagining our dates are for show makes you more comfortable, then go right ahead and believe it. As far as I'm concerned, they're to test whether or not a ninety-nine percent match is good enough."

She forced herself to stand her ground, refusing to scurry from his approach. It was tough, especially considering how her feet itched to do some fast backpedaling. But she managed. "Good enough for what?"

"To go from dating to something more."

That's what she'd been afraid of. From the start, she'd run scared. Now it turned out she'd been justified. "Maybe we could give this one date a try and not worry about the rest. In fact, if it's a really lousy date, you might not want another," she suggested hopefully.

"I agree." He swallowed her elbow with one huge hand and escorted her to the front door of his home.

"You do?" Relief washed through her, as revitalizing as a cool spring shower.

"Yup. You don't need to worry about a thing. I'll take care of all that, particularly the worrying."

"That's not what I meant," she began. Stepping across the threshold, she lost track of what she'd been saying. "Oh, my."

"Like it?"

"What's not to like?"

Cassidy looked around with hungry eyes. Now here was a home, well loved and well-worn. In the entranceway, wide, pegged-oak planks gleamed like mellowed gold in the late-afternoon sunlight. The wood was slightly trenched in places, giving evidence of generations of traffic. In front of her extended a long hallway. Off to one side she glimpsed a parlor, while off the other was a spacious living room. Above her, attached to a heavy iron chain, hung a wagon-wheel chandelier.

Ty noticed the direction of her gaze. "It came off the wagon the first Merrick bride rode in on."

"I'll bet everything around here has a history."

"Just about."

"I don't."

Ty cocked his head to one side. "You don't what?"

Cassidy indicated the pioneer antiques that dotted the parts of the house she could see. "Have a history like this."

"Everyone has a history. Some know it and some don't."

"Well, I don't." She didn't understand why she was making such an issue of it.

"Does it bother you?"

Truth vied with the need to protect herself. As usual, honesty won out. "Yes."

"Progenitor envy? I never would have thought you capable of it," he mocked lightly.

Her mouth twitched. Unable to help herself, she turned to smile at him, realizing her mistake an instant too late. He stood lounging against one of the rough-cut support pillars, looking for all the world like a gunslinger from the old West—tall, broad, lean and deadly. And resolute. Very resolute. His eyes glinted in the dusky foyer, reflecting endless patience and determination, as well as a heat more scorching than El Paso in August.

"Damn," she whispered.

He inclined his head, his comprehension instantaneous. "My thoughts exactly."

Escape became imperative, the urge driven by sheer, unadulterated panic. *Not safe, not safe, not safe!* shrieked the voices. She backed toward the door, untangling her feet as she went. "I can't do this. I thought I could, but I can't."

"You can't have dinner with me?" he asked gently.

"You know what I mean. I can't do..." Her hand darted through the air, just missing an heirloom hat rack. "This."

"Ah. Much clearer."

She glared at him. "Stop it, Ty. I don't know what you want from me. But whatever it is, I can't give it to you. Please take me home."

He hadn't moved from his position against the support post. But she noticed that all his many impressive ripples tensed. "What will you tell Hutch?"

Oh, no. Hutch. How could she have forgotten? "I'll...I'll tell him it didn't work out between us."

"You'd lie?"

That stopped her. She released her breath in a long sigh, her shoulders slumping in defeat. So much for escaping unscathed. "No."

"I didn't think so." He uncoiled from his position. "Come around back. We'll have dinner by the pool. I hope you don't mind if it's casual tonight."

She tucked a strand of hair behind her ear and smiled airily. Not that she fooled him. Oh, no. Not this guy. Not for one little minute. "Sounds great."

The pool area was dazzling and looked slightly out of place—too much for such a basic, stark environment. Slabs of various sized and hued rocks were cemented into a free-flowing patio with flowers dotting the area, some in halved whiskey barrels and others in stone planters. Mexican petunias were on the verge of blooming, while the verbena lobelia and portulaca had already flowered in a stampede of color. Off to one side was a trellised area with tables and chairs beneath. Overhead, the broad leaves of a hearty mustang grapevine provided shade. One of the tables had a gorgeous floral arrangement made up of yellow roses and baby's breath. Had he known how much she loved yellow roses, or was it in honor of his grandmother's business? Unwilling to consider the possibility they were for her, she turned her attention to the pool.

It was an amazing sight. Constructed of some sort of dark

rock, it had three levels with waterfalls flowing from one section to the other. Jagged stone slabs provided platforms for lounging on each of the levels. Thrift spilled from some of the rock ledges, the hot pink, blue and white flowers providing a brilliant floral cascade.

Overwhelmed, Cassidy didn't know what to say. "Wow" struck her as the safest comment.

"It was my father's contribution to the homestead," Ty explained dryly as they crossed to the table decorated with the roses. "The top pool is a hot tub. Useful during the summer, wouldn't you agree?"

Oh, dear. "I gather you don't use it much."

"Sure I do. I just turn off the heat and dump in a block of ice."

"Try squeezing in a bucket of lemons and adding a bag or two of sugar," she suggested brightly, taking a seat at the table. "You'll have it made."

He chuckled. "Sounds like a plan." A short, rawboned woman appeared then, carrying a tray with drinks. "Cassidy, this is Edith, my housekeeper."

Edith set a brimming glass of iced tea in front of Cassidy and a long-necked bottle of Shiner Bock beer in front of Ty. Drying her hands on her apron, she subjected Cassidy to an intent examination. An instant later, her expression relaxed and she smiled. "Willie was right. You'll do fine. Anything I can get for you, just holler. Hear?"

Cassidy couldn't decide how to answer the first part of the housekeeper's comments. As for the rest… "Thanks. I will," she finally said, deeming it the most appropriate reply.

"She doesn't mean any harm," Ty explained as soon as Edith left. "She's lived and worked here for so many years, she's become family. Unfortunately, that means she speaks her mind whether we want to hear it or not." Her expression must have been more revealing than Cassidy had intended because he sighed. "Okay, so it's a strange first date."

She let him off the hook with a laugh. "It's a relief to hear you say so. I was beginning to think the past twenty-four hours were normal for you."

He grimaced. "Yeah, right. I'm always inundated by ten-year-old brainiacs who want me to date their mothers. My grandmother is constantly computer-generating my women while my housekeeper gives them her personal stamp of approval." His mouth twisted to one side. "All they leave me to do is convince my date that she wouldn't rather be anywhere *except* with me."

If only that was true. "Well…not *anywhere*," she allowed. "There've been one or two side benefits to dating you." Including one brief instance when she'd been all too happy to curl up in his lap and let the world drift by while they shared some of the most exquisite kisses she'd ever experienced in her life. She forcibly buried the memory as deep as she could.

Apparently, it wasn't deep enough. Ty easily read her mind. Ignoring the glass Edith had provided, he hefted the beer and saluted her. "Thank heaven for ripples," he muttered, taking a long swallow directly from the bottle.

She gave him a cheeky grin. "You can say that again."

His gaze took fire, though he answered prosaically enough. "Since this isn't a normal first date, I thought we'd go over the application Hutch filled out and make sure it's right. Willie said she'd run it through the computer and see if there aren't more matches."

Cassidy choked on her tea. "More?"

"Three to half a dozen is typical. But for some reason the computer only came up with one for you."

Gazing across the flower-dotted patio, she strove for a nonchalant shrug. "Guess I'm not an easy match."

"Good."

Startled, she glanced at him. "Why is that good?"

"I don't feel like sharing."

She straightened in her chair. Uh-oh. "Look…I thought I made myself clear about this. Your kisses might knock

my socks off, but I'm not interested in any sort of relationship. Not ever. Got it?''

"Not even for Hutch?"

Ice clinked as she returned her glass to the table with
more haste than care. "That isn't fair."

"He wants a father."

"He has one. He doesn't need another."

"Then why did he turn up on Willie's doorstep?" Ty
didn't give her a chance to concoct an answer to that one.
He shoved his chair away from the table. "If you'll excuse
me, I'll get your application form and let Edith know we're
ready to eat."

Cassidy scowled at his back as he strode across the patio.
He must be aware that his leaving forced her to stew over
his parting shot. *Then why did he turn up on Willie's doorstep?* It was an excellent question. Did Hutch really want
a father so badly? He'd never said so. Of course, buying
those dates didn't leave a lot of room for misinterpretation.

She nibbled on her lower lip. Why was he suddenly so
anxious for a father? Was it something she'd done?
Something she hadn't done? She thought they were man-
aging well enough. Sure, they had to watch their pennies.
But she'd always assumed they shared the same goals.
They both were after a home of their very own and a place
to put down roots. She reached for the floral arrangement
and fingered a velvety rose petal. Not to mention a place
to grow her yellow roses.

But apparently her son wanted more. A lot more.

The instant Ty returned, she asked, "Since you have all
the answers, tell me why Hutch wants a father." Her voice
had a husky, defenseless quality she hated. Had he heard
it? She couldn't afford to betray any weaknesses. Not to
him. Not when she was already so susceptible to him.

"Most boys want a dad," he replied, dropping a folder
on a vacant chair. "Is that unreasonable?"

"Yes." The word sounded whisper soft and gut-
wrenchingly painful. Cassidy could sense him absorbing

her reply. She expected a pitying expression to creep into his eyes. To her surprise, he shrugged matter-of-factly.

"Not all men are like your ex. You should know that by now."

She shivered. Not really. After Lonnie, she hadn't allowed a man close enough to risk getting hurt again. Nor would she. She'd barely survived the five years of hell she'd called married life. If she gave her heart into another man's keeping and he walked out on her...

"I won't marry again," she stated implacably.

Ty's mouth tightened. "I know you want me to accept that as your final word on the subject." He leaned across the table toward her, spearing her with those clear, soul-deep eyes. "But I won't."

It was that kiss. That damned kiss. She'd always been brutally honest with herself and this time was no different. She preferred facing facts squarely on, and the fact was...she and Ty made for a combustive combination. From the minute he'd pulled her into his arms, she'd been lost to everything but his touch. In fact, she'd been so lost in a sexual haze, she'd even allowed him to slip his hand beneath her skirt, something she hadn't done since... Just remembering brought a hot flush to her cheeks. Of course, he noticed.

To her eternal relief, Edith's arrival prevented him from commenting. The housekeeper placed steaming hot plates piled high with green hickory-smoked ribs and pinto beans in front of them. How odd to be on the receiving end of a meal instead of the one serving it.

"Real meat," she said appreciatively, not realizing until a second too late how her comment would sound.

Ty stilled. "Is that a treat for you?"

Crud and double crud. "Yes," she admitted, scrambling for an explanation that fell somewhere between the truth and a salve for her pride. "We try to limit our consumption of red meat." Although in her case it was because of cost rather than for health reasons. "Nice weather, isn't it?" Great. That was about as subtle as a train wreck.

Edith let her off the hook by slapping a small plate on one side of the table. "Thought you might also appreciate some damp towels," she said. "So I brought those along with the napkins."

"You thought right," Ty agreed. He glanced at Cassidy, his expression more tractable than earlier. "Ribs might be messy, but they're a guaranteed icebreaker. It's hard to be formal when you're covered in barbecue sauce."

To her amazement, his comment enabled her to relax. She couldn't remember the last time a man had gone out of his way to put her at her ease. And though she might not be happy about the situation she'd been forced into, she could certainly be gracious about it. "Aren't you upset that you've been caught up in this dating mess?" Kisses aside, that was.

"If the circumstances had been different, I would've been." He gave her a level look. "If the circumstances had been different, I would've put a stop to it."

What circumstances? she wondered uneasily. Perhaps she wouldn't risk asking. "So why didn't you stop it?" she demanded instead.

"Simple. I wanted to date you."

Her breath caught. Well, that was sure frank. It also gave the exact answer she least wanted to hear. "But I saw you arguing with your grandmother about it."

He shrugged. "That was before we kissed."

Damn! Why in the world did she have to give him such an enthusiastic come-on? "It was a simple kiss, Ty. Get over it."

He actually had the nerve to laugh. "It was more than that and you know it."

Maybe. All right, definitely. That still didn't change how she felt. "I told you. I'm not interested in dating." She shoved her plate aside. "I'm through with that."

"At twenty-nine?"

Her gaze darted away again. "What does age have to do with anything?"

"You're far too young to allow one bad experience—"

"You know nothing about it!" she snapped.

"I know what Hutch told me. And if I didn't think we'd suit, I'd have told Willie to run the application again."

"Aren't you doing that anyway?"

"I'm having her rerun the form for your sake, not mine."

That brought her up short. "Oh."

"It's the truth, Cassidy."

She released her breath in a gusty sigh. "I believe you." And she did. Ty hadn't made any bones about his attraction to her. She was the one running scared, not him.

"But trust comes hard, doesn't it?"

There was no point in denying it. "Sure does."

"Then why don't we make an agreement? No shading the truth. I think it's important we be honest with one another."

She wouldn't have too much trouble with that. The truth had a way of tumbling out of her mouth whether she wanted it to or not. "Okay."

He nudged her plate back in front of her. "When we're done eating, why don't we go over that application and make sure Hutch got it right."

"Okay." Her mouth pulled to one side in a half grin and her hunger returned with a vengeance. Good gravy, had she really been about to waste all these great ribs? "Worried about that one percent?"

"Terrified."

The minute they were finished and had cleaned off the excess barbecue sauce with the damp towels Edith had supplied, Ty picked up the folder and removed a stapled packet.

"Let's take a walk while we go over the application."

"Fine." Did she sound as nervous as she felt? It had been one thing to answer Ty's questions believing he was a kid working on a science project. But to let down her guard with the man striding beside her was another matter altogether.

He handed her the papers. "Here. Start with the first page. It's just the basic statistics. Age, height, weight, educational background, hair and eye color. That sort of thing. Does it look right to you?"

She glanced over the information, slipping swiftly past the line with her age. She always winced seeing it in black and white. "How did Hutch know my weight?"

"He didn't. I guessed after meeting you."

"You're two pounds off."

He reached into his shirt pocket. "Here's a pen. Feel free to change it."

"Not much point," she admitted ruefully. "After that meal we just ate, it's probably right on the mark. Oh, and you'll have to change my occupation. I'm not a waitress anymore."

"Leave it until you see what sort of job you pick up next week."

She could hear an undercurrent of determination in his voice and sighed. "You're still resolved to help me, aren't you?"

"Yup."

"Any point in my refusing?"

"Nope. Since I'm partially responsible for your losing your job, I should help you find another."

"Partially?"

"Well…I didn't drop lunch on the guy, but I suspect I was the cause." He leaned down so his mouth came dangerously close to the side of her face. "If you hadn't been busy looking at me, you might have paid more attention to that tray."

"I—"

"Now don't go forgetting our agreement."

She frowned in confusion. "What agreement?"

"To be truthful with each other."

Her mouth snapped shut. Darn it all! How did he know

she'd been about to fib? "All right, fine. You distracted me."

"The feeling's mutual, sweetheart."

Rattled, she buried her nose in the application. "Where were we?"

"Running away?"

"Yes."

"Go right ahead. I'll catch up soon enough."

That's what she was afraid of. She scanned the next page, her attention snagging on one of the answers. "Now where did he come up with this one?"

"Which?"

She pointed. "Ideal partner. Why would he think I'd want to date a cowboy?"

"I believe Hutch said that was the only type you hadn't tried before," Ty replied in neutral tones.

"*What*?"

He lifted an eyebrow. "A small misunderstanding?"

"To put it mildly. Oh!" She began to laugh. "Oh, dear. I think I see."

"Care to clue me in?"

"It's Hutch's dad. Lonnie was something of an expert at trying out different fields of endeavor. I believe at the time of our divorce the only type of employment he *hadn't* tried was wrangling."

Ty's mouth curved upward—a most attractive sight. "Got it."

She glanced at the sheet again and promptly choked. "Pet peeves...April Mae. I swear I'm going to kill that kid."

"Would you care to change it?"

"Yes! Where'd that pen go?" He recovered it from his shirt pocket and handed it over. "Turn around." Using his broad back as a table, she took perverse pleasure in scratching out April Mae's name and scribbling in "liars".

"Hey, easy. You already ruined one shirt today."

"Oh, sorry."

"Done?"

She forced herself to step away, fighting the temptation to linger over the broad, sweeping planes of his back and all those lovely, irresistible ripples. Yum. "Okay. I'm through."

He twisted around. "I think the rest of the questions were ones you answered on the phone. But you might want to give them a quick check, just to be sure."

She scanned the last few pages. "Looks fine to me."

"In that case, I'll give Willie the changes and let her run it again."

"Is that it, then?"

"Not quite. There's one more detail we still need to check out."

"What?"

"This."

She should have seen the kiss coming. Or perhaps she had and pretended otherwise. So much for absolute honesty. Just as before, she dove into the kiss with an enthusiasm he couldn't mistake. With a soft groan, he responded with equal zeal. Why did this keep happening? Cassidy wondered helplessly. She should be shoving him away, not clinging like moss to a rock.

The image seemed appropriate, though—soft on hard, flourishing in a place no life should be possible. Ty offered her heat where for so long she'd only known cold. He gave freely of himself rather than doling out affection in grudging nuggets. He'd never shown annoyance with her clumsiness or accused her of gracelessness. He hadn't even thought it. If he had, she'd have heard it rumble through his dark voice or seen it slip across his expression. She'd have sensed his impatience or distaste.

Instead, all he'd ever betrayed had been a stark desire, followed by an immutable determination to put his stamp on her, to claim her as his. She'd never experienced that before. And despite herself, she found it all too compelling.

She wanted to be loved to the exclusion of every other woman, just as she wanted to love as completely in return.

Love.

She ripped her mouth from Ty's, fighting for breath. Where the heck had that word come from? "I can't do this," she whispered, escaping from his arms in a whirlwind of hands, elbows and knees.

For a large man, he moved with amazing agility, escaping serious injury thanks to hair-trigger reflexes. "Easy, sweetheart, easy," he soothed. "It was just a kiss."

"If that's all it was, I wouldn't be overreacting like this," she argued, despising the small quiver fluttering through her voice. It made her sound unbearably vulnerable.

Gentle laughter glittered in his pale eyes. "Then you admit it was more than a simple kiss?"

She scowled. Somehow he'd tricked her. She wasn't quite sure how, but retreat seemed the best option. "I'd like to go home now, if you don't mind."

"Fine," he readily agreed, which only ticked her off all the more. No doubt he felt he'd won a major victory in their dating war. She wished he didn't appear so smug about it. Or so incredibly enticing.

Put a damper on it, girl!

And she tried. She sincerely tried the entire way home. But she fast came to the conclusion that the only thing guaranteed to ease her hunger would be to leave the feast. And that meant leaving Ty. The instant they reached her apartment complex, Cassidy jumped from the pickup, only to be brought up short at the steps to her building. Hutch sat on the stoop, a scruffy mop resting in a tangled heap beside him.

"I blew it, Mom," he began.

With a muffled groan, she turned to face Ty, not in the least surprised to find he'd followed her. "Looks like we're going to have to change that application form again," she warned.

"Really?" His calm reaction washed over her like a balm. "Why's that?"

She pressed her lips together to keep them from trembling. "We've just been evicted."

Progress Report

I told Mrs. Welch she didn't have to watch me after all. I wanted to get everything done without her figuring out what I was up to. I have to shut the computer down for a day or two, so I'm making a few last notes until I'm on-line again. Plan B has been set in motion and everything's proceeding right on schedule. Mom's due home any minute, so I have to get going. Want to be downstairs when she arrives. I wrote up my plan for Experiment #2, just in case this all works out. I know it's a bit premature, but—

Oops. The landlady's banging on the door. Gotta go.

CHAPTER FIVE

Experiment #2: Relocation
Goal: Okay, this is gonna be tricky. If Ty's protective instincts check out, he'll take care of Mom when she loses the apartment. I'm hoping he'll take us home with him. Of course, Mom is gonna say no. So I'll just have to find a way of making her agree without her realizing I'm behind it.
Procedure: Limit Mom's options so she has to let Ty help whether she likes it or not!

EVICTED. Cassidy didn't wrap it up in pretty words, Ty noted. Although how pretty she could have wrapped an eviction notice he couldn't quite imagine. His brows drew together as he considered her situation. What sort of sorry SOB would toss a helpless woman and child out on the streets in the middle of the night?

"You've been evicted?" Ty demanded of Hutch. "You sure?"

At the boy's confirming nod, Cassidy's shoulders slumped for a fraction of a second. Then she stiffened her spine and set her jaw. "Okay. We can deal with this."

"So that's where he gets it," Ty murmured.

She turned dark eyes in his direction. "Pardon me?"

He made a fist and lightly tapped her rounded chin. "Hutch always sticks his out, too. I gather it's a family trait." He'd knocked her off balance with his comment, which gave him a chance to address Hutch. "What happened?"

"Our landlady, Mrs. Walters, saw me with Miz Mopsey."

"Who?"

At the sound of her name, the mop beside Hutch shifted ever so slightly so that the tangle of off-white strings poofed out as if they'd been zapped with an electric charge. The dog offered a halfhearted, guilty-sounding bark. Hutch patted what might have been the head. "Animals aren't allowed here, so we've been keeping her secret."

Ty lifted an eyebrow. "Jeez, it's a dog. Who'd have guessed."

Hutch scuffed his toe. "I'm sorry, Mom. Mrs. Walters caught me sneaking the mop out for a walk and made me pack everything up. We have to leave *now*."

"She can't do that. It's illegal," Ty stated. "Why don't I talk to her?"

"*No!*" Hutch erupted off the step. "She…she was mean. I don't want to live here anymore. She wouldn't let Miz Mopsey stay inside even for one night. So we don't have any choice. We have to leave. Right away."

Right away, huh? Interesting. Ty folded his arms across his chest and did some jaw-setting of his own. "Trust me. I can change her mind."

Beside him, Cassidy stirred. "Thanks all the same, but this isn't your problem. It's mine. And it isn't just Miz Mopsey. We're also behind on the rent."

"I suspect that's my fault, too," he retorted, all the while keeping his gaze fixed on a red-faced Hutch. "You couldn't have earned much tip money today, thanks to me."

"No, I didn't," she conceded. "But it wouldn't have made that much difference. I had some unexpected car expenses this month, too. It put us behind."

"Still… The woman shouldn't have made Hutch sit out here on the stoop."

"To be honest," Hutch began—a first since they'd arrived, Ty was willing to bet, "it's Miz Mopsey who has to stay on the stoop. Not me. I was afraid to leave her alone, so I decided to sit with her until you got back."

"What about Mrs. Welch? Why isn't she still watching you?" Cassidy asked.

"I...uh...told her you'd just pulled up."

"You know better than that," she scolded, though clearly, her heart wasn't in the reprimand. "I'll go in and start packing."

"No need. I took care of everything." Hutch smiled angelically. "I didn't want you to have any more hassles after what you've been through today. So I packed everything up and stashed it right inside the door."

She leaned down and ruffled his hair, offering a tremulous smile. "Thanks, sweetpea. I don't know what I'd do without you."

"I could make a wild guess," Ty muttered.

She swiveled to frown at him. "What did you say?"

He attempted to match Hutch's innocent smile. "I said, I'd like to have you as my guests." He wasn't the least surprised when she shook her head.

"Thanks, but that's not necessary." Her tone was adamant. "We'll stay in a motel for a night or two while I look for a new place."

He could press the issue but suspected it wouldn't get him anywhere. Cassidy Lonigan might have a voice like sweet syrup, but it covered an indomitable will. Backing her in a corner would only force her to fight all the harder for her freedom. She didn't wait for his reply but opened the door to the apartment building and picked up the first of the boxes stacked inside. Clumping down the steps, she tripped along the sidewalk toward a rusted-out rattletrap. Watching her, Ty didn't know whether to laugh or pack the woman up in one of her own boxes and dump her in his truck. Following her example seemed the smartest choice for now. He climbed the steps and selected the largest of the cartons stacked by the door. Passing Hutch, he surprised a scowl on the boy's face.

"What's with you, kid?"

"Nothin'."

Yeah, right. It didn't take more than half a brain cell to figure out what was bothering the boy. "You don't know your mother real well, do you?"

That got a reaction. "Course I do! She's my mom."

"Then you ought to know what would happen if I insisted the two of you come home with me. Now get your butt off that stoop and grab a box."

By the time he and Hutch had reached Cassidy's bucket of bolts, she was on her way back for a second load. "She'd keep sayin' no," the boy said as they stowed the boxes in the car.

Ty suppressed a grin. So the kid had been paying attention. "And if I kept pushing her?"

"She'd tell you no, come hell or high water."

"Watch your mouth, boy."

"Yes, sir. Sorry."

Seeing that at least Hutch's contrition was sincere—if little else—Ty relented. "If there's one thing I've learned about your mother, it's that she's prideful and as self-sufficient as they come. I might not like the decisions those traits cause her to make, but I respect your mother too much to try to impose my will on her. It's her choice or no choice. So until we find a way to coax her down our pathway while keeping her pride and independence intact, we back off. Let her check out all the other available trails first. With luck, she'll eventually see things our way."

Hutch beamed. "No problem. I think I can get her on the right path."

"Now why doesn't that surprise me?" Ty muttered.

"Because you know I'm smart. Scary smart." The boy adjusted his glasses and fixed Ty with serious blue eyes. "And that doesn't bother you, right?"

Ty snorted. "Not hardly."

Something akin to relief crept into the boy's gaze. "Just checking. You could have changed your mind since earlier."

"I haven't and I won't. Now, do we have that settled once and for all?"

"Yeah."

Ty jerked his head toward Cassidy, who was lugging two scraggly potted rosebushes—nary a leaf or bud in sight—down the sidewalk. "Then shake a leg. We can't let your mom do all the work."

It didn't take long to load the boxes that contained the sum total of the Lonigans' meager possessions. With the exception of the computer, which had been carefully stashed by Hutch on the back seat, it was a pitiful collection. Even so, one large box didn't fit, no matter how many times Cassidy tried to force it.

"It's the books," she said to Hutch. "Maybe we should leave them for Mrs. Walters to donate to the library."

Ty folded his arms across his chest. "Or you could ask me to hold on to them until you're settled into your new place."

"I really don't want to impose..." she began, then ground to a halt. Something in his expression must have given a hint to the anger smoldering inside. With a quiet word of thanks, she turned the carton over to him. "I'll let you know where we end up."

"No need. I'll follow you to the motel."

"That's not necessary..." She released a gusty sigh. "You're going to pull the man thing, aren't you?"

"If you mean, am I going to make sure you get to a motel safely, then yes, I'm pulling the man thing." He eyed her vehicle in disgust. "Considering your car—and I use that term loosely—is held together by rust and sheer faith, it's the least I can do. And, no doubt, the least you'll allow me to do."

To his intense satisfaction, her expression revealed a hint of consternation. "Thank you," she murmured again. "I owe you. Come on, Hutch. Climb in."

To Ty's amusement, the boy didn't utter a single word of protest. Nor did he offer any words of farewell.

Interesting. Sudden suspicion held Ty in place. Sure enough, when Cassidy turned the key in the ignition, nothing happened. Not a cough. Not a whimper. Not even a bellow of smoke and gasping death rattle.

"Gosh, Mom," he heard Hutch exclaim. "What's wrong?"

"I...I don't know."

"Well, pop the hood and let me take a look."

Burying his amusement, Ty braced his shoulder against a convenient tree trunk and waited. Hutch climbed out, Miz Mopsey in tow. Cassidy joined them at the front of the car. She opened the hood and locked it in place while her son climbed onto the fender and peered into the greasy mass of wires and steel. Ty bit back a shout of laughter as the dog wriggled her way up beside the boy, snuffling beneath the hood as though offering her opinion on the matter.

"Need help?" he called, knowing before he even spoke what the answer would be.

"No, thanks," Hutch hastened to reply. "I see what it is." He glanced over his shoulder at his mother. "It's the caliper switch. Burned clean out."

She sighed. "Crud. Can it be fixed?"

"Not tonight."

Ty strolled over for a peek. Never having heard of a caliper switch, he was curious to see what the kid had done to the car. It only took a second to discover that the battery had been disconnected. He slanted a glance at Cassidy. She was totally oblivious. No question, mechanics weren't one of her strong points. Fortunately, mind-blowing kisses were.

"Sure you don't want some help?" he offered casually.

"Oh, no. Hutch can deal with it," Cassidy insisted.

Ty shrugged. "Okay by me." Hell if he'd argue. If she'd asked, he'd have told her the truth about the battery. But since she chose to be stubborn, she could suffer the consequences—especially since those consequences worked to his advantage.

"Well, darn." She ran a hand through her hair, turning the straight, dark sheet into an attractive tumble. "I wonder how expensive caliper switches are?"

That brought him up short. "I don't expect the repairs will cost you much at all," he hastened to reassure her. He'd be damned if he'd let the kid add to her financial worries.

"Really?" Relief surged through her voice.

"At the risk of stepping on your independent nature, could I offer you a place to stay tonight?" He strove for humble and came within spitting distance of it. "I have a cabin between the main house and the bunkhouse that's not in use."

"Oh." She brightened at that little tidbit. "That would be lovely. How much is the rent?"

White hot anger shot through him. He managed to control it through sheer dint of will. Barely. "Maybe you better take Miz Mopsey and go wait in the pickup," he advised softly. "Hutch and I will move everything over."

"But—"

"Now."

Her eyes widened in alarm and he knew it was just dawning on her that he was a hairbreadth away from thoroughly losing his temper. "Are you upset about something?"

"I'd be happy to discuss it with you another time."

She planted her hands on her hips, compelling him to jump clear of her elbows. "Is it because I wouldn't go home with you initially?"

Since Cassidy was intent on discussing this out on the sidewalk, he'd empty the pasture. No point in innocent bystanders getting injured in the ruckus when they locked horns. Ty caught Hutch's eye and jerked his thumb toward the pickup. "Hutch, you wait in the truck with Miz Mopsey."

Hutch looked from one to the other with interest. "You and Mom gonna fight?"

"Discuss, boy. We're discussin' the situation."

"You might want to discuss, but I've seen Mom like this before. She wants to fight."

"*Hutch*!" Cassidy and Ty rapped out in unison.

"Fine. But you're not fooling me." Hutch stared pointedly at Ty. "I warned you I was smart. It doesn't take a mental giant to see you two are ready to rumble." With that astute observation, he gathered up his dog and trotted toward the pickup.

"There. See what you've done?"

Ty drew a deep breath. Patience. If he could just manage to hang on to his patience, he'd have the future Mrs. Merrick safely almost-tucked in his house. The cabin was just a few short steps away. No doubt an excuse would arise that would bounce the stubborn woman from there into his arms—and into his bed.

"Apparently, my eyesight isn't that great," he allowed, hustling Cassidy to the far side of the tree he'd been leaning against—and more importantly, out from under Hutch's watchful eye. "What have I done?"

"You've upset my son."

"Your son is not upset."

"You made me yell at him."

"He handled it amazingly well."

"I *never* yell at him."

"He'll live. Now, are you going to help load these boxes, or would you rather wait in the truck with Hutch?"

Her chin made a reappearance, poking in his direction. "I think it would be best if you drop us off at a motel."

He'd had all he could take. Striking with a speed that would have done a rattler proud, he snagged her around the waist and yanked her up against him. He avoided her pinwheeling arms and a wayward knee with practiced ease. Her size ten sandals were another matter. Why the hell did the heels on women's shoes have to be so damned pointy? Fortunately, his boots were tough and her accidently tromping on him didn't hurt much more than when he'd broken his leg. He decided to ignore the crunching pain, especially since kissing her made it well worthwhile.

Their mouths collided, then joined in complete accord. Her lips were soft and moist beneath his, eagerly parting at the touch of his tongue. She wrapped around him with all the warmth of lamb's wool on a frigid night and he returned the favor by easing into her with the same sigh he used slipping into a steaming hot tub after a hard day of wrangling.

His reaction to her touch was stronger than before. The closest he'd come to the sensation was when he'd slammed back a double shot of whiskey. The liquor-driven wildfire had shot from his throat straight to his gut and left him feeling both powerful and sucker punched, all at the same time.

Cassidy hit harder still. She also brought out every primitive instinct he possessed and every protective one, as well. He needed her in his life with a desperation he couldn't mistake. Now all he had to do was convince her that she burned just as fiercely for him.

He pressed her against the tree trunk, leaning into her. Hell, he fell into her. His mouth moved more forcefully on hers and he filled his hands with her soft, plump breasts, thumbing the kerneled tips. She must have liked it. With a low groan, her nails climbed his back, carving deep, loving half-moons into his flesh. She even stopped grinding into his toe long enough to clip his ankle, wrapping a long leg around his. He only prayed he lived long enough for her to love him to death in bed.

The honking of a nearby truck horn forced him to release her.

She stared up at him, her gray eyes silver in the moonlight. "Are you trying to kiss me into submission?"

"Is it working?"

She hesitated. The instant he started to lower his head again, she broke into speech. "I think that was Hutch honking. Maybe we'd better load those boxes."

"And where am I taking you?"

She cleared her throat, offering a tentative smile. "Would you be willing to put us up for a day or two?"

"And how much is the rent?"

"I believe..." She moistened her lips—plump, damp, delicious lips. Lips still carrying his taste, he was willing to bet. "I believe you offered to have us as your guests."

"Now was that so hard?"

"I'm not used to having someone else in control. I'm usually the one who manages everything."

"You think I'm trying to take over, is that it?"

"It sure feels that way."

"Well, I'm not. I admire strong women. Hell, Willie's about as tough as they come. The only time you'll get a fight from me is when you're choosing the most difficult path just to be ornery."

"Going to a motel was not—" One look in his direction and she broke off what she'd been about to say and closed her mouth. Skirting the tree, she grabbed her precious rosebushes from the trunk of the car and trotted toward his pickup.

"At least life will never be dull," he muttered to himself.

Depositing the potted bushes in the bed of Ty's truck, Cassidy glanced at him over her shoulder, offering a dazzling smile. Uh-oh. "I have an idea. I can help around the ranch in exchange for room and board. How about that?"

He restrained himself from responding. It was tough, but he did it. "Nope," he said beneath his breath. "It'll play hell with my self-restraint, but it won't be the least dull."

Ty stood at the door of the cabin, his arms folded across his chest. "How did this happen?"

"I'm sorry, Ty," Hutch said with a big show of contrition. "I musta left the door open when I took our clothes over to your laundry room. I guess the stupid critter snuck right in. Thank goodness we hadn't unpacked your pickup yet."

Cassidy sniffed, her expression clearly one of disgust. "A skunk!"

"Don't scrunch up your face like that, Mom," Hutch whispered. "It'll give you wrinkles."

Ty's foreman, Lorenzo, stuck his head in the doorway, then swiftly withdrew. "Damnedest thing I ever heard of, boss."

"Isn't it though." Ty pinned his gaze on the shuffling ten-year-old beside him.

"There are six different types of skunks indigenous to Texas, you know," Hutch volunteered, a hint of anxiety creeping into his voice. He fingered his glasses, nudging them higher on the bridge of his nose. "It coulda been a western spotted skunk. They favor rocky bluffs like this area around here."

"Think so?" Ty asked very, very softly.

"Maybe." The boy blinked rapidly. "I know it wouldn't be the eastern spotted. We're too far west for them. Or the hooded skunk. They're pretty darned rare. And they tend to be farther south, as I recall."

"You seem to recall quite a bit."

"Well, I do remember a few facts from the books I've read. Like…" He swallowed, darting Ty a nervous glance before doggedly continuing. "Like it could also have been a striped skunk. 'Cept they'd rather be in the woods."

"You read some weird books, kid," Lorenzo offered. "Ever tried comics?"

"No, sir. Not since I was three. As for the skunk…it could also be the common hog-nosed."

"Don't have any rooter skunks around here," the foreman explained kindly. "Wonder what made him spray?"

Ty fixed his gaze on his soon-to-be son. "Or why he'd be out exploring during the day. Most skunks are nocturnal."

Hutch swallowed visibly. "Gosh. Who knows? Maybe he has insomnia. That might have made him upset enough to spray."

Ty glanced at Cassidy, his mouth tightening into a grim line. She looked like hell. No doubt she felt like it, too. Right now, she carried the weight of the world on her shoulders and this latest incident was one more crisis she didn't need.

"Did it ruin anything?" she asked, tension vibrating through her voice.

"We were real lucky, Mom. None of our clothes got it since we had all that wash to do. And I hadn't unpacked my computer yet."

"Or much of the truck, by the look of things." Ty stepped through the doorway of the cabin and inhaled deeply. The pungent aroma had already started to dissipate. Interesting. He'd never known skunk stink to be quite so accommodating. "Guess that only leaves us with one option."

Cassidy nodded stoically. "Sure does. If you wouldn't mind driving us to a motel, I'd be grateful."

"No! We can't! I mean—" Hutch broke off and shrugged awkwardly. "I was hoping we could move into the bunkhouse instead. I've never stayed in one before. It sure would be educational."

Ty shook his head. "No way. That's a men-only bunkhouse. And your mom doesn't come close to qualifying."

"Oh," Hutch said with a return of last night's angelic innocence. "Where could *she* stay? Hey! I know. How about in the main house?"

"I don't think—" Cassidy began.

"Great idea." Ty gave Hutch a hearty slap on the back. To his credit, the boy only staggered a little. "Cassidy, you can stay up at the main house, and Hutch can sleep in the bunkhouse with the wranglers. Hope you like getting up early, kid. My men roll out around five-thirty."

"Five," Lorenzo corrected with a wicked grin. "And since you're off for spring break, *chico*, you can lend us a hand. See what wrangling's really about. What do you say?"

Ty didn't wait for the little genius to come up with an excuse. "Glad we have that settled. Lorenzo, get some of the men to move these boxes up to the main house. Hutch, you lend a hand."

"I'm not sure about this," Cassidy tried again.

"What could be better?" Ty wrapped an arm around her shoulders. "You'll have a place to stay while you look for an apartment and a new job. And we can get all those pesky dates out of the way. It's a win-win situation."

"I guess...."

"Would you mind helping Edith direct traffic? She'll show you the rooms you can use and you can tell the men which boxes go where."

She brightened right up, just as he'd hoped. Figured. No doubt she found the idea of telling people where to put things too appealing to resist. Oh, yeah. It was going to be a very interesting marriage. He slanted Hutch a quick look. Once he explained who was in charge of this little party. He caught the boy by the scruff of his neck before he could scamper off, ignoring his desperate little wiggles to break free.

"While you help Edith, I'll get Hutch settled," he informed Cassidy with a winning smile, praying she wouldn't notice her son squirming beneath his hold. She didn't, and the minute she'd escaped hearing range, he addressed her son. "Give it up, boy. You might be able to talk rings around half of Texas, but you don't have a prayer of talking your way from under my hand."

Hutch scuffed a well-worn sneaker in the dirt, the fight draining clean out of him. "Okay. I won't run."

"You have something to tell me, boy?"

"Yes, sir."

"Get to it."

"It wasn't a skunk that made that smell. I did it with some chemicals."

"You mean you lied. Again."

Hutch gulped. "Yes, sir."

"What did I tell you about lying?"

"You don't abide it."

"No, I don't. You have something more to tell me?"

Hutch attempted a smile, the angelic devil back for an encore. "I don't understand. What do you mean?"

"Don't bother shoveling that line of bull with me. Unlike your mother, I know a cowpatty when I'm about to tromp through it. I'm talking about the apartment and the car."

Hutch's face collapsed into lines of defeat. "We were evicted. Honest. That much is true. But…" His chin wobbled briefly before he brought it under rigid control. "But only after I walked Miz Mopsey past Mrs. Walters's door once or twice. Or maybe a bit more."

Ty bit down on his tongue. Hard. "What about your mom's car?"

"I disconnected the battery cables," Hutch whispered.

"Why?"

"So you'd take us home with you. That way, you and Mom could…you know."

"Oh, I know all right. But you sure as hell shouldn't."

Ty thumbed his Stetson to the back of his head as he mulled over his options. He had half a mind to clue Cassidy in on the whole sad story. But the stress he'd seen lining her face gave him pause. If he told, pride would force her into a motel. Not only would it add to her financial burden, but…damn it all. He'd only just gotten her here. He didn't want her leaving. So, what the hell should he do?

Hutch echoed Ty's thoughts. "What are you going to do?"

"If I was smart, I'd tell your mother about all the stunts you've pulled."

"Hey, Ty? Since you don't mind that I'm smart, I don't mind if you aren't," Hutch offered generously.

Ty suppressed a laugh. Fixing a fierce scowl on his face, he said, "Don't get cocky, kid. That's three times you've hung me up with your lie. There better not be a fourth incident or you'll live to regret it."

"No, sir. There won't be." Hutch peeked up at him, for the first time looking far younger than his ten years. "Are you going to punish me?"

"There'll be consequences, that's for sure." Maybe if he kept the boy busy, he wouldn't have time for mischief. Doubtful, but it wouldn't hurt to try. "First, get that cabin aired out. Then clean it from top to bottom. Edith will tell you where to find the supplies."

"I'll take care of it right away. Anything else?"

"Yeah. Just to make certain you don't have the energy to come up with any more clever ideas, the next two weeks you're going to learn all about wrangling. Lorenzo will be happy to teach you."

Hutch grinned. "I can? Really?"

"Don't get too excited. It's hard work and long hours."

The boy shrugged. "I'm used to that," he said with heart-tugging sincerity. "I don't mind."

"Tell me that at the end of the two weeks and I might believe you. And finally, I want your word of honor that you're through lying."

"I am. I promise."

"Not so fast." Ty propped his size fifteen boot on the first step of the cabin and leaned down so he and Hutch were at eye level. "You take a minute to think about what I'm asking. A man's word might be all he has to offer someone. You don't give it lightly. And once given, you stick to it, no matter how tough it might prove to be."

Hutch stared solemnly through the glinting lenses of his glasses. "No fudging, huh?"

"None."

"Okay. I give you my word. I won't tell any more lies."

"Fair enough." Ty held out his hand, engulfing the boy's in a man-to-man shake. To his surprise, Hutch didn't rush off but stood shuffling his feet some more. "All right, kid, spill it," he prompted with a sigh.

"Well..." The boy adjusted his glasses for a moment

before continuing. "Since we're being so honest, I think there's something you should know."

Just great. One more lie to keep from Cassidy. "What's that?" he asked warily.

"It's about the reason I bought Mom those dates...."

Ty waited, not quite sure where this latest confession was headed.

"You see...I went to Miss Willie's because I wanted to get myself a dad," Hutch revealed in a rush.

Okay, that wasn't so bad. It merely confirmed what Ty had long suspected. "Yeah, I guessed as much. I wouldn't consider that a lie, so don't sweat it."

"Thanks, but there's another reason I bought Mom all those dates."

That figured. "Go on."

It took three more minutes of foot scuffing and throat clearing before Hutch managed to spit it out. "Mom's planning on moving back to Georgia."

Damn. "I hope you're joking, kid."

"I wish I was. You see, Mom's aunt and uncle live there. They're the ones who raised her. When she got married, they weren't real happy about what she'd done. But now she wants to move back there so she can mend fences and put down roots. At least that's what she said."

Ty swore beneath his breath. He'd hoped to have time to slowly court Cassidy, to break down the barriers she'd spent so many years erecting. But it looked like their leisurely courtship was about to turn into a whirlwind romance. And unfortunately, it would take a hell of a lot more than sweet talk and kisses to persuade a certain wary divorcée to walk down the aisle with him. She wouldn't be easily wooed back into the marriage bed, no doubt about that.

"When's she planning to move?" he demanded.

"As soon as she's saved enough money to make the drive and completed one last goal she set for herself."

"Goal? What goal?"

Hutch shrugged. "Never said. But I know it's important."

"Okay. Thanks for warning me. I'll take care of it."

"What are you going to do?"

Ty glanced toward the main house and sighed. "Why don't you let me worry about that particular problem? Maybe I can offer her some incentive to stay put for a while."

"Sure you don't need my help?"

Ty managed to contain his response to a simple, unequivocal, "Positive."

"I don't know," Hutch said morosely. "Once Mom's made up her mind, it's real tough to get her to change it. She can be pretty darned stubborn."

"Yeah, well, I can be pretty darned persuasive. In case you weren't aware, gentle persuasion has moved many a stubborn mule."

Hutch's pale brows drew together. "What if that doesn't work?"

"Then I'll hog-tie her to a fence rail until she sees reason."

And chances were good he'd have to do precisely that.

Progress Report

I'm back on-line now and the experiments were a success. Ty did just what I hoped. You know...he's okay. He's kinda tough, but fair. Even when he found out what I'd done, he didn't yell or anything. And he didn't treat me like a kid, even though he keeps calling me that. He's punishing me for lying, but that's okay. Except for having to clean the cabin, the punishment is gonna be fun. I always wanted to be a cowboy, even if it's only for a couple of weeks.

Oh! And I told him about Georgia. Boy, was he mad. But at least he knows. Maybe now he can stop her.

I don't want to move to Georgia. I want to stay in Texas. I want to stay with Ty.

The truth is...I want Ty to be my dad.

CHAPTER SIX

Experiment #3: Living at Ty's + Romantic Situations = Love

Goal: I think people fall in love faster when they hang around together a lot. Now, Mom won't go for that. She's really good at saying no! And Ty seems to want to take it slow for some stupid reason. So I'll have to find ways to hurry them along if I'm gonna have a dad before I turn fifty!

Procedure: Get them in places where they'll want to kiss. (Yuck!)

TY CONFRONTED Cassidy across the generous expanse of his office. "The hell with gentle persuasion! I should have known it would never work with you," he bellowed. So much for broaching this subject with delicacy and tact. "Now, what do you mean you're moving to Georgia?"

The hell with gentle persuasion? Where had that come from and what did it have to do with her impending move? "What's wrong with Georgia?" Cassidy bellowed right back, grateful for the solid door separating Ty's office from the rest of the house. With luck, it would limit the number of people overhearing their "discussion". Well...with a *lot* of luck.

He glared at her for an endless moment before muttering, "I don't live there and neither should you."

Her lips twitched and her anger faded as swiftly as it had risen. "Do you realize how ridiculous that sounds?"

Unfortunately, while her annoyance had ebbed, his had intensified. He booted a leather ottoman out of his path and came to loom over her. Not that she let him get away with

107

it. Heck, no! She shoved her nose to within inches of his and glared back.

"I'm ridiculous?" he demanded. "Why? Because I want you to stay here? Because I'm willing to admit there might be something happening between us, while you're intent on running away?"

He knew just which buttons to push to ignite her temper. "I'm not running away." She fought to lower her voice. "I'm going home."

"Home?" That stopped him. "Why didn't you mention this before?"

"I…" Good question. Why hadn't she? Maybe she hadn't said anything because she suspected he'd react precisely like this. Or maybe she'd kept quiet because she'd taken one too many pages from Lonnie's book on how to sneak away without anyone knowing. "It didn't come up," she said, airing the excuse with a hint of bravado.

Not that he swallowed it. "Bull. We agreed to be honest with each other, remember? Now give it to me straight. Why are you moving to Georgia? I thought you'd told me you didn't have a heritage or roots or a home like mine."

"I don't. Not really. I guess you could say Georgia is as close to a home as I've ever had."

Home. How odd that sounded. She'd never thought she'd call her old neighborhood by that name again. Not in this lifetime. But if she reconciled with Aunt Esther and Uncle Ben, she and Hutch would have family and roots. They'd finally belong instead of being tossed to and fro across Texas like hapless tumbleweeds. She could stop running.

"You still consider Georgia in those terms—as home—even after a ten-year absence?"

Not really. "Of course."

"You have family there?"

"An aunt and uncle," she admitted. "We've exchanged a number of letters recently and they've indicated that they'd like me to come back. They want to get to know Hutch and put our problems behind us. They're not as young as they used to be and I'm not sure how much longer they can manage on their own.'' She gave a helpless shrug. ''It seems right somehow.''

''To mend fences and put down roots.''

''I see you've been talking to Hutch.''

Ty ran a hand across the back of his neck. ''A bit. I can tell you he's not anxious to leave Texas.'' His eyes glittered with undisguised frustration. ''I'm not anxious for you to leave, either.''

Why did she have the uncontrollable urge to throw herself into his arms and confess her desire to remain right where she was? Why did the idea of returning to Georgia suddenly feel so very wrong? And why did a part of her continue to fight so darned hard to deny those urges?

''That decision was made long before we met.''

''And now that we *have* met?'' He dropped his hands to her shoulders, enclosing her in warmth. It was a warmth she wanted to inhale clear down to her soul, a revitalizing warmth like a fragrant summer breeze on a starlit night. It carried the whisper of promises kept and hope renewed and a fathomless, endless love. ''Now that we've touched each other, now that we've kissed?''

She shivered, caught by those dueling urges. The one continued its strident demand that she find a home in his arms and never leave, while the other replayed the history of her last botched love affair. Her only love affair. The voices of fear won and she pulled free of his grasp, surrendering ground in order to distance herself from him. She tripped over the poor abused leather ottoman in her haste and it rolled drunkenly on its side.

''Look...'' She lifted her chin, attempting to project a calm control she didn't feel. ''I left home under unfortunate circumstances—''

''You got married. Sure, it didn't work out, but at least you—''

''I was pregnant.'' The truth escaped in a rush.

That brought him up short. ''A shotgun marriage?''

"Not really. My aunt and uncle didn't want me to marry at all. They thought I should have the baby and put him up for adoption. Instead, I took off and married Lonnie."

"Does Hutch know?"

She shook her head. "I haven't mentioned it. If he'd ever asked, I'd have been frank with him." She gave a self-conscious shrug. "There's not much point in lying. All he has to do is check the date on my marriage certificate against his birthday. Since there's only seven months between the two, it doesn't take a lot of brain power to figure out what happened."

Compassion turned his eyes to jade. "No. I can't see Hutch being easily fooled."

"Nor would I want to fool him." She wrapped her arms around her waist, aware of how telling the defensive gesture must appear. "For all Lonnie's faults, he did the honorable thing by me back then. It wasn't easy for him. He's a runner by nature and it must have taken a lot of guts to marry me when every instinct urged him to grab the first bus out of town."

"So why did he run after five years? Why hang in there so long?"

Cassidy firmed her lips, praying Ty wouldn't notice how they trembled. But to this day, the memories skulked in the far recesses of her mind like shadowy nightmares. "He didn't hang in there. He ran at the first opportunity—one short month before Hutch's birth, to be exact."

"The month *before*..." Comprehension dawned, along with a deep, burning anger, an anger directed squarely at Lonnie. "And you spent the next five years chasing after him."

Hearing it stated out loud made her decision seem downright pathetic. But she'd been so young and so scared. And so desperately broke. Pride had come last in a long list of needs—a list Hutch had topped, just as he topped it now. "Something like that."

"What stopped you from following him? April Mae?"

"No. I could have dealt with that. But he hurt Hutch, said unforgivable things. And that made me realize that no father was better than a bad one." By that time, she'd also discovered that she could scrape by on her own.

"I'm sorry, Cassidy. You must know that not all men are like Lonnie. Some of us have staying power."

A knock at the door saved her from answering. Edith poked her head into the room and glowered at them. "Dinner's on," she announced. "Miss Willie arrived while you two were having your little discussion. When she heard the set-to goin' on in here, she decided to wait in the dining room with young Hutch. She asked for a drink. A strong one. And the boy asked for one, too. Gave him the most powerful lemonade I had on hand. If we don't eat soon, the sugar rush is like to knock him loopy."

Ty nodded. "Go ahead and serve the meal. We'll be right there." The second the door slammed behind her, he turned to Cassidy. "This discussion isn't over yet."

"It is as far as I'm concerned." She kicked the upended ottoman back into position. To her surprise, Ty leaped out of the way. Jeez. No need to overreact. It wasn't as if she was aiming at him or anything. "Now that Hutch has told you about Georgia, you can understand that a relationship between us would be impossible."

"We'll see," was all he said. "Shall we eat?"

"I could use the fortification," she muttered.

A quick grin slashed across his face. "Stoking up for our next battle?"

"Something like that."

"Oh, don't worry. I'll keep you well fed." He waited until she swept past before adding, "Not that it'll do you any good. This is one war I intend to win."

To Cassidy's relief, dinner turned out to be a delight. Willie entertained them with stories of her dating agency and the various matches they'd made, particularly her most recent ones. "Autumn and Clay were already crazy about each other," she explained. "They were just too stubborn to realize it."

Cassidy cupped her chin in her palm and smiled wistfully. "But you got them to see the light?"

"Not me," Willie denied. "I have to give Maria credit for that one. She knew how to handle those two. And don't forget Cody and Emily."

"Not to mention that damned magazine article," Ty inserted in annoyed tones.

"What article?" Cassidy questioned, thoroughly confused.

"Now, Ty, don't fuss. Emily didn't know they were going to do a hatchet job on us. That was the magazine editor's fault. Fortunately, Wanda saw through all the lies and ended up making the perfect match, without even using the—" Willie broke off with a laugh and inclined her head toward Hutch. "Good gracious. I think it's time a certain young man turned in."

Startled, Cassidy glanced at her son. He'd nodded off at some point, his cheek pillowed by an uneaten pile of mashed potatoes. His glasses sat cockeyed on his face, making him appear far younger than ten and infinitely more vulnerable than when he was awake and busily manipulating the world around him and the hapless mortals peopling it. Beneath his chair, Miz Mopsey snored delicately, apparently as exhausted as her master.

"I'll carry him to one of the spare bedrooms," Ty offered. "I think the bunkhouse better wait one more night."

Cassidy pushed back her chair. "Thanks. I don't know what's wrong with him. I've never seen him so worn out. You'd think he'd spent the whole day working instead of exploring the ranch."

Inexplicably, Ty chuckled. "Oh, I suspect he found a chore or two to keep him busy. Get used to it, Cassidy. Ranch life might be a bit more physically strenuous than he's used to, but it won't hurt him."

Her maternal concern faded. "I'm sure you're right. In

fact, it'll probably be good for him." She watched as Ty levered her son onto his shoulder. Scrawny arms crept around his neck and clung. For some reason, the sight brought tears to her eyes. She cleared her throat, hoping no one would notice how husky her voice had grown. "He doesn't get out in the fresh air as much as I'd like."

"Don't tell me we're in agreement about something?" Ty demanded. "You're willing to admit that ranch life is good for the boy?"

She wrinkled her nose at his teasing. "I suppose that ninety-nine percent had to kick in sometime."

"Ninety-nine point four," Willie corrected, her tone reflecting intense satisfaction.

Cassidy turned, surprising a smug expression on the older woman's face. "Excuse me?"

"I reran your form with the alterations Ty gave me and it came up ninety-nine point four percent this time. It seems the changes improved your odds."

Oh, great! "Well, maybe…" she conceded. "But there's still that one percent difference."

"Point six," Ty corrected, gently digging potatoes out of Hutch's ear and wiping gravy off his cheek. "And closing all the time."

"According to the computer," Cassidy pointed out before addressing Willie again. "I don't suppose your machine made any additional matches?"

"Nope. Looks like you're still stuck with my grandson." She lifted her glass and winked. "Better the devil you know, I always say."

"Hey! Whose side are you on?" Ty protested.

No question about that. Clearly, Miss Willie approved the match as much as Ty and Hutch. Which left her standing all alone and defenseless—not to mention tempted beyond endurance to buckle beneath their not-so-subtle pressure. "What would you have done if there'd been other matches?" Cassidy asked.

A lazy grin crept across his mouth as he started to leave

the dining room. She gave chase, curious to hear his answer. "I'd have invited them up to the ranch," he explained as he headed down a long hallway. "That way, I could have checked them out before they dated you."

Yeah, right. "Don't you mean scared them off?"

He shoved open the bedroom door next to hers. "That, too."

"I don't get it. Why are you so certain we'd make a good match?" She turned down the bed and stepped out of the way so Ty could lower her son to the crisp cotton sheets. "I mean, it can't really be because the computer said so."

He tugged off Hutch's sneakers and jeans and then removed his glasses, gently setting the wire rims on the nightstand. "It isn't."

She moistened her lips, steeling herself to ask the question that had been plaguing her since yesterday. "It's that kiss, isn't it?"

"Yes." With infinite care—more care than she'd ever seen Lonnie display—Ty pulled the sheet over Hutch and tucked it around the boy's sleeping form. "Didn't you feel it, too?"

She preceded him across the room and switched out the lights. "That's just a physical response," she replied in an undertone. "Hardly enough to base a serious relationship on." She should know. She'd fallen into that trap once before.

He pulled Hutch's door closed. "It's a start."

She shied away from the eventual outcome that predicted. Why couldn't she get across that she wasn't interested in a long-term affair? Heck. She wasn't even interested in a short-term one. "But there's more, isn't there? More than just a kiss."

He hesitated in the darkened hallway. "I guess you'd call it a family tradition."

"Kissing?" she asked in disbelief.

A broad smile slid across his bronzed face. "That's right."

"Interesting tradition."

"Oh, it gets even more interesting." He propped his shoulder against the wall and captured her hand, drawing her to a halt. "You see, according to legend, the Merricks always know their soul mates when they finally meet."

Not safe! In a replay of their first meeting, the words shrieked in her head, threatening to deafen her. But she was helpless to resist his comment or the inexorable pull on her hand. "How do you know?" she demanded.

"The same way you knew. It only took one kiss."

Panic darkened her eyes to slate. "No. Don't say that."

"It's only fair that I tell you the truth."

Fair? What was fair about any of this? Her response to his kisses wasn't fair. Hutch's desperation to have a father wasn't, either. But least fair of all was her uncontrollable reaction to Ty, a reaction that echoed his and that grew more intense with each hour in his company. "You don't understand. I'm not interested in dating."

"You got that part across loud and clear. The question that remains is…why?" He tilted his head to one side. "I've heard Hutch's opinion on the matter. What I haven't heard is yours." He paused a beat. "But not tonight, I don't think. You look exhausted."

He'd let her off the hook and ironically enough he did it at the very moment she was tempted to crawl into his arms and tell him everything. She really must be exhausted. "I think I should turn in now." *Ask me to stay.*

He feathered a hand along her cheek. "Anytime you want to talk, I'll be here for you."

"Thanks. Please say good-night to your grandmother for me." She took a deep breath, almost drowning in the scent of him. Using every scrap of strength she possessed, she turned away. After all, her independence was more important than anything.

Right?

* * *

Cassidy glanced around the room Ty had assigned her and released a sigh that was half beatific and half sorrowful. This one room was larger than her entire apartment—and that didn't even include the attached bathroom. The tub alone could hold the navy's Pacific fleet with room to spare for a yacht or two.

Clipping her ankles as she attempted to skirt the haphazardly stacked boxes, she dug through the smallest of the cartons for her scrapbook. Next to her rosebushes, it was her most prized possession.

She managed to unearth the overstuffed book and carried it to the huge four-poster bed, dropping it onto the mattress. It did a lovely little bounce before scattering a few odd mementos across the spread. To her amusement, one of them was a note she'd written, praising her last apartment for being so roomy. Of course, without furniture to clutter up the place, a shoe box would seem spacious.

Stripping off her clothes, she dug through another box for her nightgown. Pulling on the slip of cotton, she returned to the bed and plopped down beside her scrapbook. "Plopping" proved to be her undoing. For some inexplicable reason, landing so solidly on the bed was one more mistake in the multitude that comprised her life.

The bed collapsed at one end and the mattress tilted against the wall, sending her and the scrapbook cartwheeling toward the headboard. She banged against the heavy oak frame and was instantly buried beneath an endless cascade of downy pillows and soft cotton bedding. With a muffled shriek, she kicked her legs to try to free herself from her cocoon. Not that it did much good, since her feet were sticking straight up in the air.

The next thing she knew, the door ricocheted open. There was an instant of absolute silence, broken by a half-smothered chuckle.

"Don't you dare laugh!" she ordered crossly.

"Sorry." She heard Ty's leisurely tread as he approached. A second later, he peered down at her with an expression of careful inquiry. "Need help?"

With all her heart, she wished she could refuse. Considering she was practically standing on her head, her dignity spared only by the fortuitous drape of a sheet, she didn't dare brush him off. She glared at her toes for several long seconds as she weighed wisdom against pride. Too bad she hadn't been able to spare the extra couple bucks to purchase an eye-catching red polish for her toenails, she thought irritably. Maybe it would have distracted him just a tad. But, no. They were as naked and exposed as the rest of her and he wasn't the least bit distracted. Her dilemma held his full attention.

Crud.

"Yes, I could use your help," she said, surrendering with a sigh. "If you wouldn't mind."

"My pleasure." He reached down and slipped his hands beneath her arms, carefully lifting her free of her predicament. To her relief, he also snagged the sheet, so her assets remained well protected. "Should I bother asking what happened?"

She grimaced, carefully draping herself in crisp cream-colored cotton, her scandalously naked toes peeking out from beneath the improvised robe. "It's your bed. You tell me."

"Give me a minute." He stripped away the rest of the bedding, including the pillows. Her poor scrapbook had scattered across the floor and he worked cautiously around it. "Looks like the rails have been disconnected from the headboard. You're lucky the whole thing didn't collapse on top of you."

She eyed the heavy piece of carved oak and winced. That would have hurt. "How did the rails get disconnected?"

He gathered up the small pile of bolts he'd unearthed beneath the bed. "I assume with a wrench."

She stared in bewilderment. "But…why?"

"When I find out, so will you. In the meantime, I'll get the tools I need to reassemble the bed."

Before he could act, the door flew open and Hutch stood there, Miz Mopsey at his heels. "Something woke me up," he said, making a big production of rubbing his eyes. The dog barked her annoyance, too.

"Sorry about that, sweetpea," Cassidy said. "My bed collapsed."

"Oh." His attention switched to Ty. "What are you doing here?"

"I came to help your mom."

"Oh," Hutch said again. "You were rescuing her, huh? That's really cool. Isn't that cool, Mom? You have somebody to rescue you now. You've never had someone do that before, have you?"

Ty folded his arms across his chest and fixed a certain young troublemaker with a piercing gaze. "Why do I have the impression we need to have another discussion, boy? I don't suppose you know how this bed got derailed."

To Cassidy's surprise, Hutch began scuffing his toe against the carpet and hemming and hawing. She groaned. "Oh, Hutch! You didn't."

Hutch swallowed. "I think I'm really sleepy now." He gave an exaggerated yawn. "I better get back to bed. Come on, Mops."

"Good idea," Ty inserted smoothly. "Good night."

The instant Hutch and his dog disappeared, Cassidy turned on Ty. "You don't really believe he unbolted the rails?"

"Sure do."

"But...*why*?"

"You heard him. He wants to turn me into some sort of knight in shining armor. I'm supposed to rescue you."

"Not a chance..." She stumbled to a halt. Was it possible? A week ago, she'd have sworn the idea of Hutch's buying her a date was ludicrous. But he had. Perhaps he'd taken this dating nonsense one step further. Perhaps now he was angling for a— "Oh, no."

Ty cocked an eyebrow. "Change your mind?"

"It's…it's possible," she conceded.

"I believe the word is 'probable'. Give me a minute to find a wrench and pliers and we'll have your bed back together in no time."

He returned so quickly she'd only had a chance to pull on a robe and start gathering up the various papers that had come loose from her scrapbook. He immediately stooped to help. She wished he hadn't. He knelt too close and smelled too good. And those ripples were bothering her again, too. They strained against his shirt each time he reached for a piece of paper. Ignoring him didn't help. Nor did closing her eyes. Unable to see, she couldn't get her scrapbook collected with a speed that was fast becoming a necessity. Even worse, with her eyes closed, she shut all the delicious sights and sounds inside where her mind could play them over and over in every delectable detail.

"So what's all this?" he rumbled at her.

She risked a quick peek at what he held. "Just stuff I've kept over the years." She strove to sound casual. But with him hanging all over the top of her, it was difficult. "You know. Feel-good stuff. Like a gratitude journal."

He frowned at the slip of paper. "'The rose clipping I gave Mrs. Walters bloomed today,'" he read. "'It's great that someone is getting flowers from my bushes.' That made you feel good?"

"Well, sure…" Her brows drew together. "I wouldn't have had any roses if I hadn't let Mrs. Walters take a clipping."

"But you didn't get the flowers. She did."

Cassidy hated when he used logic on her. Did he have any idea how difficult it was some weeks to find the positives in her life? That particular day, the roses were the one bright spot in twenty-four hours of unbearable darkness. "I got to share in the pleasure of them," she argued.

Sort of. At least Mrs. Walters had let her see the pretty yellow bloom when she'd knocked on the door to brag about it.

Ty picked up another scrap of paper. "'We had meat today. Not the kind you have to stew for hours, either. But real, honest-to-goodness'..." His voice trailed off. "Aw, honey..."

"Don't." She moistened her lips. "Don't pity me. It's okay to be poor, you know." She gave him a crooked smile. "It makes you appreciate the small things."

"Like having ribs at lunch the other day."

"Yeah. Like that."

His mouth compressed. "And like this? 'Freddie canned me today, but I sure am grateful that he let me work for so many months.' You're grateful to him? He fired you!"

"But he hired me in the first place," she pointed out. "He didn't have to do that. He was very tolerant, especially considering how many dishes I broke. It's a wonder I didn't put him out of business through breakage alone."

"Uh-huh. And for today I suppose you'll put in there about how grateful you are that Hutch unbolted your bed rails."

Her chin crept out. "Maybe." Then she released her breath in a sigh. "No. I don't think that's going to make it into my scrapbook. I'm really sorry about this, Ty. I'll speak to him in the morning."

"Don't worry about it." He retrieved the final piece of paper and handed it to her before turning his attention to the bed. "Why don't you let me talk to him?"

"Don't bother. He's my son. I can handle it."

"I'm sure you can. But I suspect this is one of those occasions when a man's touch is called for. Will you let me discuss it with him?"

Cassidy hesitated. Boy, oh boy, did she want to refuse. He glanced up at her from his reclining position on the floor. Good gravy, he was big! Big, male and sexy as the dickens—with a wrench in one hand, a collection of bolts

in the other and a smile that promised a sinfully delicious
night. She couldn't remember the last time that particular
combination had been in her bedroom. Now that she
thought about it, she'd never had anything like Ty anywhere close to her bed.

"You can talk to him," she reluctantly agreed.

"Why the hesitation? Am I stepping on toes?"

At the reminder, she frowned at her unvarnished toenails,
wiggling them as she considered. Was he treading where
he didn't belong? Did that explain her reluctance? Or was
it because with each day that passed, he became more and
more intricately locked into their lives? Soon she'd be leaving Texas. The minute she accomplished the one final goal
she'd set for herself, she and Hutch would gas up the car
Ty disparagingly referred to as a rattletrap, load it with all
their belongings and limp eastward toward Georgia. Once
there, they'd mend fences with Aunt Esther and Uncle Ben
and sink their parched roots into rich, red Georgia clay.
There wasn't room in her plan for a six-foot-four-inch
Texas rancher with enticing green eyes and a come-to-bed
smile.

Ty climbed to his feet and approached. His huge, steel-
tipped boots stopped scant inches from the end of the bare
toes she'd been contemplating. "You haven't answered."

"I'm thinking."

He stooped so she was staring at the top of his head.
Streaks of sun-kissed gold threaded through his light brown
hair, tempting her to slip her fingers through the richness.
"Okay," he demanded. "Which toe was I stepping on?"

"Excuse me?"

He pointed to her big toe, grazing the unpainted tip.
"The 'this is my problem and I'll handle it' toe?"

She shivered at his touch. "Nope. Not that one."

His finger tickled the next in line. "Maybe it's the 'I
don't want to be obligated' toe. No, wait. How about this
little fella? The one I affectionately call 'Remember the
Alamo'. The toe of death before surrender."

A smile slipped across her mouth. "Not that one, either."

"Hmm. That only leaves two more." He tapped the next in line. "It can't be the prideful toe. No need in this case. Which leaves this teeny one at the end. The 'he's getting too involved and we're leaving for Georgia soon' toe. Right?"

"Bingo," she whispered.

"So that's the little troublemaker." He reached into his back pocket and pulled out the pliers he'd been using on the bed. "I can take care of that problem easily enough. Now hold reeeeal still."

"Oh, no, you don't!" With a shriek of laughter, she danced around him and leaped toward the bed.

"No, wait," he exclaimed an instant too late. "I only fixed the one—"

She was in midair when the warning reached her. She hit the mattress solidly. As she bounced up, the mattress and box spring collapsed in one corner. Her second bounce sent her rolling in a tangled ball of arms and legs toward the corner of the headboard again, her skull cracking on the solid oak. Her backside wedged into the tiny cubbyhole formed between the dipping mattress and the headboard.

"Rail," Ty finished with a sigh.

"Now you tell me. Gosh. What pretty stars."

Ty was on top of her in an instant. "Hang in there, sweetheart. I'll have you out in a sec." Behind them the door banged open.

"You're rescuing her again," Hutch announced in delighted tones. Miz Mopsey barked her delight, too. "I'll bet you've never been rescued twice in one day, have you, Mom? I'll bet you like it a bunch, don't you?"

"*Hutch*!" Ty and Cassidy shouted in unison.

The only response was the scamper of feet and pitter-patter of paws rapidly retreating down the hallway.

"I know you're partial to that kid," Ty said, popping her free. "But I'm afraid I'm gonna have to kill him."

She yanked her nightgown back into position and retied her robe. "No problem," she said, shoving hair from her eyes. "I'll help you." They glanced at each other, sharing a moment of perfect accord, their annoyance giving way to laughter.

"He's a challenge, that's for damned sure. Fortunately for you, I love a good challenge." Ty shifted the headboard and slipped the last rail into place. "Give me a second to bolt this together and you should be safe enough."

She frowned. "I have to tell you. The floor is looking better and better."

He resumed his position beneath the bed and went to work with his wrench. "Or you can join me in my room."

Say what? Where had that come from? "Sure," she scoffed, trying to sound offhand. "That's just the sort of complication we need now."

"You're right. It is." The wrench hit the floor with a clatter. "In fact, I've got an even better complication. How about marriage?"

"Marriage!" She blanched. "Who said anything about that?"

"I did." Slowly, he climbed to his feet. "And just so you know…I'm gonna keep saying it until you agree. So. Will you marry me, Cassidy?"

"That's impossible," she whispered.

"Is that your answer?"

"Please don't do this."

"Is that your answer?"

"Yes!"

He grinned. "Yes?"

"No! Yes, my answer is no." She folded her arms across her chest and scowled at him. "I can't marry you."

"Okay." He collected his wrench. "Today's answer is no. We'll see what it is tomorrow."

Hadn't he been listening? "It'll be no tomorrow, too."

"That's one possibility. Of course, there's another."

"What's that?" she asked apprehensively.

He paused at the door. "I could get lucky. Tomorrow you could tumble into my arms like a hot jalapeño, ripe for the plucking, and beg to be mine."

"Yeah, right. In your dreams."

His green eyes seemed to catch fire, burning her with their intensity. "There, too," he said. And then he was gone.

Progress Report

Well, it's not going quite as smoothly as I'd hoped. I thought maybe Mom would like having Ty come to her rescue. Instead, they were just mad that I disconnected the rails. But I'm not giving up yet. I still have another idea how to get Mom married off. I'll just make sure Ty gives her all the things she likes best. All the things a dad should remember to give a mom. The kind of stuff that makes her cry cuz she's happy, not cry cuz she's sad.

CHAPTER SEVEN

Experiments #4–7: The Great Mom and Ty Experiments
Goal: To set up situations where Mom and Ty will be
alone so they can get to know each other better and get
the 99.4% part of their match working instead of wor-
rying so much about that stupid .6% difference. (Mom
sure does fuss about that a lot!)
Procedure: Have Ty give Mom all the nice stuff and
good times Lonnie never did.

"GRAB a shovel and start digging a hole right over there
by the porch steps," Ty said, pointing. "And I'll dig one
on this side."

A very subdued Hutch nodded his compliance. "Yes,
sir."

Ty let him work his hole for a while before speaking
again. "So what happened last night?"

"You mean with Mom's bed?"

Cute. "Yeah, that's what I mean."

"I...uh...unbolted it."

"You want to tell me why?"

"So you could rescue her." Hutch wiped the sweat from
his brow, his expression earnest. "Nobody's ever saved her
before. Not until you came along."

"I appreciate that, but—"

"This way, Mom can be like a fairy-tale princess." He
beamed. "Girls like that kind of stuff, don't they? I don't
think she's ever been a princess before."

No, she hadn't. At least, not judging by the bits and
pieces he'd gleaned from her scrapbook. Still... The kid
better stick a sock in it, or the princess was going to load

her glass slippers into her rusty pumpkin carriage and high-tail it to Georgia. And the good ol' prince would be minus a wife, minus a son and living unhappily ever after.

"I appreciate your help, Hutch. But it's time for me to take over now. Your mom could've been hurt last night. You wouldn't have liked that, would you?"

Hutch shook his head. "No way! I didn't mean to hurt her."

"I think you should tell her that, not me." Ty dumped fertilizer and topsoil into his hole. "Okay, bring me one of those rosebushes."

"How come we're planting them?"

"Because otherwise they're going to die. And I don't want to see your mom's expression if that should happen."

"Heck, no." Hanging over the hole, Hutch watched Ty carefully smooth dirt around the roots. "You're hoping they'll grow some flowers, aren't you?"

"Yup. I'm hoping once she sees how well her roses grow in Texas soil, she'll decide to plant her own roots here, too."

Hutch nodded his approval. "Good idea."

"I thought so." Ty rocked back on his heels and tipped his Stetson off his forehead. "But these roses are going to need time to grow. You can't rush 'em. Do you read me? Do you understand what I'm saying?"

Hutch released a long, drawn-out sigh. "You want me to stop helping you and Mom?"

Ty suppressed a grin. "You're quick, kid. I always did like that about you." He removed his gloves and shoved them into his back pocket. "I don't mind your helping, so long as I ask for it first. Okay?"

"I guess." Hutch adjusted his glasses. "You sure I can't help just a *little*?"

"Now that you mention it, I could use some." Ty nodded toward the side of the house. "Why don't you grab the hose and give these bushes a drink?"

* * *

Ty caught Cassidy going through her wallet a few days later, counting out the piddling stack of bills that were undoubtedly all she had left to her name. From his vantage point, the few there were carried good ol' George Washington's enigmatic smile. Not pleasant to be down to a handful of one dollar bills. Desperation would undoubtedly follow close behind and Cassidy desperate wasn't a sight he cared to witness, any more than her reaction should her precious roses die now that he'd planted them.

Then he thought of something and roundly cursed himself for a fool. They were supposed to have picked up her paycheck from the café. With all the craziness of the past several days, he'd forgotten about it—although he'd remembered to retrieve her car and reconnect the battery cables. He'd also taken a few minutes to have an intriguing discussion with Cassidy's former landlady. What he'd do with the information he'd gleaned, he hadn't quite decided.

His mouth slanted in a wry smile. No question about it. Once he convinced the love of his life to join him in holy matrimony, he'd have his hands full with their ingenious— not to mention devious—son. At least their conversation a few days ago had helped. Ever since they'd planted the rosebushes, Hutch had been on his best behavior.

"Ty?" Cassidy caught up with him on the porch, a worried frown lining her brow. He longed to smooth it away, to ease her fears and concerns and allow her to concentrate on the pleasures life offered instead of fighting for sheer survival. Unfortunately, she wouldn't let him. Not yet, at any rate.

"What can I do for you, sweetheart?"

She'd stopped protesting his use of endearments, although they were almost guaranteed to bring a flush to her cheeks. "I need to go into San Antonio for the day."

"Would you like a lift? I'd be happy to drive you there."

She avoided his eyes. "That's not necessary. I'll take my car. I have…things to do."

"Things." What sort of things? he couldn't help but

wonder. Not that he couldn't guess. No doubt they were independent things. Things guaranteed to put as much distance between them and raise as many barriers as she could manage.

This time, she did glance at him, her gaze direct and forthright. "I have to get a job and find a new place to live, as you're well aware."

Uh-oh. "You agreed to stay here as my guest until after our Fiesta date," he reminded in his mildest tone of voice. It was one of the few concessions he'd wrangled out of her.

She looked like she wanted to argue. Being a smart woman, she thought better of it. "You're right, I did. But in the meantime, I have an appointment I can't miss."

His relief was tempered by concern. "You feeling okay?"

A smile eased the strain he read in her eyes. "It's not that sort of appointment. It's a project I've been working on. A long-standing one. And if I don't make it there today, I might not get around to it again any time soon." She took a deep breath. "So it's now or never."

She didn't explain further and he knew better than to push, though her determination intensified his curiosity. He might want to insist she share every aspect of her life with him, to trust him with all the intimate details. But that would have to wait until she was ready. "Sounds like it's important to you," he limited himself to observing.

"Very. It's a project I've been working on for some time now." She glanced toward the bunkhouse. "The thing is…I'm going to be back late and I wondered if you'd mind keeping an eye on Hutch."

"You know that's not a problem. Sure I can't give you a lift?"

Her chin came into play, settling along lines that warned he'd lose this particular argument should he choose to turn it into one. "Thanks, but this is something I have to take care of myself."

He inclined his head. "Think you'll be home for dinner?"

She didn't call him on his use of the word "home". Instead, she checked her watch. "I should be. If not, I'll phone."

With that, she trotted over to her car, spent a good three minutes wrestling the door open, climbed in, banged her head on the frame and spent another three minutes tugging it closed. The car started with a sputtering grumble and she disappeared down his driveway in a plume of dust and exhaust. Well, at least he'd filled her gas tank—filled it nice and full so she could drive long and far.

He shook his head in disgust. How damned charitable of him.

It was late when Cassidy returned to the ranch and she was starving. Her appointment had taken nearly eight hours and her mind—what little remained of it—was numb. She'd called to warn she'd miss dinner and Ty had promised to save her some. She stood just inside the front door and absorbed the ageless silence of the hallway, comforted by the sheer solidness of her surroundings, welcomed by the whispers of the past that filled every nook and cranny of the homestead. And she relaxed for the first time in weeks.

She'd come home.

"Ty?" she called.

"In here."

His voice came from the direction of his office and she crossed the hallway to hesitate outside the half-closed door. Pushing it open, she stared in disbelief. Everywhere she looked were baskets and vases overflowing with yellow roses. In the middle of the room, he'd set a table for two. Silver glistened in the subdued lighting, while crystal and wafer-thin porcelain gleamed. Best of all, the wineglasses were brimming with a rich red Cabernet Sauvignon. Next to the table stood a cart with the most delectable aromas she'd ever inhaled wafting from beneath covered dishes.

It took a moment to find her voice. "What's all this?" she asked, although it seemed obvious enough.

Ty offered a lopsided grin, one as irresistible as it was endearing. "It's for you. Edith and I figured you'd be wiped by the time you got in. And since moving to the ranch has forced an extra couple hours' drive on you whenever you have to go into San Antonio..." He trailed off with a shrug. "Besides, it gets us started on those dates."

Tears pricked her eyes. They had to be from exhaustion since she wasn't one to cry when someone acted this incredibly sweet. Although, if she was honest, she'd admit that she couldn't remember the last time someone had taken care of her like this. Cosseted her. Made her feel special.

He crossed to her side, standing so close his woodsy scent became a part of her. "Are you crying?" he asked.

She shook her head in instant denial. "I can't be. I never cry."

His laugh slipped around her, as warm as an embrace, and he reached out to catch a tear with his knuckle. "Well then, you've sprung a leak. You've got all this wet stuff spurting out of your eyes."

Reluctant amusement fought with the tears she'd denied. "This is the end of March. I'm sure it's just a spring shower."

"No doubt," he said gently. "Hungry?"

"Famished."

"Sit down and we'll eat."

"You waited for me?"

"I didn't want you to eat alone."

"Thanks," she whispered, unbearably moved. She hesitated by the table and her hand crept out to finger the white damask tablecloth. "I could get used to this."

"I'm counting on it."

The urge to flee overwhelmed her, just as it infuriated her. Where did these feelings come from? She wasn't Lonnie, to run at the first hint of commitment, was she? And though she valued her independence, Ty hadn't tried to steal that from her. Anyhow, not so far. He might propose once a day, but he took her refusals in stride and with good humor. In fact, he teased her unmercifully, promising to get even when she finally broke down and accepted his marriage proposal.

"Give me a second to wash up," she requested. And to get herself under control.

"Take your time. I'll have the salad and appetizer ready to go as soon as you get back."

"An appetizer? I'm impressed." Her tears slowed and she even managed to achieve a light tone. Not that she fooled him. But at least he didn't say anything her pride could take exception to. "I'll be right back."

She used the powder room at the end of the hall. Standing in front of the mirror that hung over the washbasin, she scolded herself for a good five minutes. What the heck was she so afraid of? Why couldn't she accept the small kindnesses Ty offered with a modicum of the grace Aunt Esther had drummed into her? It didn't mean she owed him or had to pay him back for his generosity. Her mouth twisted. Nor did she have to marry him, no matter how much she might—

Oh, no. Her eyes widened in disbelief. That wasn't possible. She couldn't have fallen for Ty. Not so soon, and not after all she'd been through with Lonnie. Hadn't she learned her lesson the hard way? Hadn't she learned that men loved women until it became inconvenient or until the responsibilities became too much? Or until someone better came along?

But Ty isn't Lonnie, the voices inside her head insisted. Darn those nasty, illogical *wrong-thinking* voices. Sure, Ty seemed a different type than her ex-husband. But she had Hutch to worry about. She couldn't risk the heartache that would follow if her relationship with Ty didn't work out. Because if it didn't, she wouldn't just lose a husband this time.

Tears burned her eyes again. This was Merrick land. Any

roots she put down would have to be yanked up and re-planted elsewhere. Considering how fragile those roots had become—as fragile as her poor rosebushes—she doubted she could survive another transplant.

Besides, she'd come so close to achieving the goals she'd set for herself five long years ago. She'd proven that she could be a good mother to Hutch, that she could support and raise him on her own. She'd learned to stand on her own two feet, to depend on no one but herself. She'd even contacted her aunt and uncle and discovered that they were as heartsick at the manner in which they'd parted as she was. And she'd taken the final step toward her most important goal, getting her—

A soft knock sounded on the door. "Honey? You fall asleep in there?"

She sniffed. "No."

"Everything okay?"

"No." She rested her forehead against the oak panel and splayed her hand across the cool wood. As a substitute for Ty's warm arms, it lacked a great deal. "Not really."

"Anything I can do?" So understanding. So gentle. So loving.

So tempting.

"Those voices are talking to me again."

There was a long silence. "The ones you told to shut up when we first met?" he asked cautiously.

"Yeah. Those ones."

"What are they telling you?" Apprehension grated his voice.

"That you're not Lonnie."

That perked him up. "Hey! I'm beginning to like those voices."

"Oh, really? They're also the ones that told me to sleep with my ex before we got married."

"Ah. I see the problem."

She swiped the tears from her cheeks. That darned spring

shower had turned into a summer torrent. "So now I don't know what to do."

"How about opening the door and having some dinner? We can decide whether the voices have me pegged right another time."

She opened the door a crack. "You don't understand. That's the problem."

He stood just outside the doorway, smiling down at her, his eyes so full of love it hurt to look at him. "What's the problem, sweetheart?"

"How can I possibly trust them when they were so wrong before?"

He cupped her damp cheekbone. "Maybe they've gotten older and wiser since then. It can happen to the best of us."

She hadn't thought of that and it cheered her immensely. "I think I'm hungry now."

"Great. Let's eat. I'll light the candles so I don't see all the wrinkles Hutch claims you have and we'll stuff ourselves until we can't move."

A laugh broke from her. "He told you about the wrinkles, huh?"

"He's even the one who suggested the candlelight."

"Lovely." She joined Ty in the hallway. "One of these days that kid's going to go too far."

"I suspect that day's right around the bend."

They entered his office and he gestured toward the table. "Have a seat. There's salad and homemade tortilla chips to go with Lorenzo's personal salsa. Then for the main course we have—"

The lights winked off just as Ty pulled out her chair. She took a stumbling step forward, tangled with the chair leg and plunged full force against him. He hadn't anticipated the blow. He went over liked a felled tree, carrying her with him. He also managed to snag the tablecloth on the way down. Dishes and silverware, flowers and food pelted them as they hit the floor with Ty flat on his back and Cassidy riding on top.

"Are you hurt?" he questioned urgently, running his hands over her, checking for damage.

She lifted her head and looked around. Not that it helped. The room was pitch-black. "I...I don't think so. What happened?"

"The power must have gone out." He groaned, shifting beneath her.

"What about you? Are you okay?" Alarm filled her and it was her turn to check him for damage. As far as she could tell, everything seemed intact. At least, all his ripples were where they belonged. "What's wrong?"

"There's salsa and chips sliding down my neck."

"Really?" Her stomach growled. "I could probably help with that," she offered diffidently.

"What the hell are you doing? Damn it, Cassidy! Are you *eating* off me?"

"I'm hungry." She held a broken chip to his mouth. "Want some?"

"Oh, I want some all right."

Tossing the chip aside, he thrust his hands into her hair and found her mouth with amazing accuracy. Salsa mingled with a flavor so inviting, so delectable, that she could easily spend a lifetime savoring it. Her lips parted and she practically inhaled him. His tongue swept inward, a welcome invasion. He groaned again, but she suspected that this time it had nothing whatsoever to do with the salsa dripping down his neck.

She reached up and cupped his face. Blind, she could only trace the hard, sculpted lines. His brow was broad, his cheekbones high and taut. And his lips... She skimmed them with her callused fingers, only then realizing how abrasive her touch must feel. "Am I being too rough?" she asked in concern, whipping her hands away from his face.

His laugh was smothered against her mouth. "Not hardly. Why?"

"My hands. They're..." She shrugged, the movement scraping her breasts across his chest. "You know."

"You've worked hard, sweetheart." His hands covered hers and he returned them to his face. "But we're a matched set in that department. Haven't you noticed?"

For some reason, his observation filled her with delight. "You're right. We are."

"We match in other ways, too."

Her sigh filled the air. "What ways?"

"Let me show you." His legs parted slightly so she slipped into the angled notch they formed, his hips cradling the most feminine part of her. He eased his hands up the length of her spine, pressing her so close she could feel each lovely ripple of the muscles supporting her. "See how well we fit together?"

"You can't be comfortable with me draped all over you," she protested.

"You don't get it, do you? You're perfect. You fit me better than any woman I've ever known." He held her close, made love to her with his mouth and his hands and his gentle, rumbly voice. "As far as I'm concerned, you can drape yourself over me any day of the week. You can drape yourself over me when the snow flies, or when it's hotter than Hades, or when the day's been tough or life's been unfair. If you need someplace to go, my arms are waiting. They're always open for you, sweetheart. When we're old and gray and I'm not as strong as I used to be, my arms will still have one purpose. And that'll be to hold you."

Tears mingled with the salsa dripping on his neck. "Oh, Ty."

He released a rough laugh. "Why I want to marry a woman who does so damned much leaking, I'll never know. Except that I do." He gathered her up, kissing her senseless and then kissing her some more. "Get ready for today's marriage proposal, love. If you can resist a man flat on his back covered in salsa and chips, you're the stubbornest woman I ever have met. But here goes—"

Somewhere behind them, a door banged open and a

flashlight beam played across the devastation of the room. Eventually, it landed on them and wobbled violently. "Oh, golly," came a breathless voice.

Cassidy tried to squirm out of Ty's arms, but he held her fast. "Hutch? Is that you?"

"Whatcha doin' down there, Mom?"

"The power went out and I couldn't see where I was going, so I tripped."

She could actually hear his gulp. "But...where's your candles? You were supposed to have candles."

Ty shifted beneath her. "Boy, if I discover you had something to do with the power cutting out, there'll be hell to pay! You got that?"

"Uh-huh." The door banged shut and ten-year old feet scampered down the hallway. Two minutes later, the lights flickered back on.

Ty helped Cassidy stand. Lettuce, salsa, roses and wine spattered his formerly cream-colored carpet. "Damnation," he muttered. "Watch the broken dishes. I guess we should be glad we weren't cut."

Cassidy eyed the wrecked room in undisguised horror. This was all her fault. Why had she ever agreed to stay here? It had been a mistake from start to finish. "I'll pay to replace everything that shattered and arrange to have your carpet cleaned."

He shot her an infuriated glance. "If you value your life, don't go there. I don't expect you to pay for a damned thing. Clear?"

She studied the glittering shards of their wineglasses dotting the carpet. "Clear as Waterford crystal."

"I'll have a little chat with Hutch in the morning and get this nonsense straightened out. In the meantime, I think there's a dish or two on the cart that hasn't been dumped. Why don't we shower and meet back down here in ten minutes?"

Sensing it was wiser to agree than argue, she acquiesced

with a nod. "Though I would like to suggest we try paper plates."

There was a moment of absolute silence and then a reluctant laugh from Ty. "With plastic knives and forks?"

She grinned. "And foam cups for the wine."

He gave her a gentle push toward the door. "Go on and get cleaned up. And don't worry about the mess, okay?"

"I'll try not to worry *too* much." She hesitated in the doorway. "By the way…thanks for filling up the gas tank. It was sweet of you."

"I didn't want you to run out," he said with more than a touch of irony. It only took a second for her to catch the double meaning.

The instant she had, she did precisely that. She ran.

"What do you mean, we've run out?" Cassidy coasted her car to the side of the road in the nick of time. The engine gave a final coughing sputter and died. "How can we be out of gas? I topped off the tank on my way back from San Antonio three days ago."

"Let's see, three days ago…" Ty frowned in mock concentration. "Oh, right. That would've been the day you went into town to do…*things*, as I recall."

She folded her arms across her chest and locked gazes with him. "Exactly. *Things*."

"Well, one of the *things* you might have considered doing was filling up the tank." Ty pointed at the gauge, flicking it with his finger. "When that needle points to the big *E*, it means you're sucking fumes. Or didn't Hutch ever explain that to you?"

"Oh! I'm telling you I topped off the tank on my way back to the ranch," she argued. "I should have a full tank. See that *F* at the top of the dial? Hutch told me that means full and that's what the damn tank should be."

He grinned at her sarcasm. "Why, I do believe my sweet Southern belle just said a naughty word."

"Damn it all, see what you made me do? I never swear."

"It's all my fault, right?"

"Hey, you're the one who insisted we take my car into town."

"With good reason, if memory serves. I wanted my mechanic to check it out while we picked up groceries for Edith. If you're still bent on driving this thing all the way to Georgia, I'd feel a lot better if it had a chance of actually getting you there."

"Thanks a lot. Instead we're out of gas in the middle of nowhere like a couple of teenagers on their first date." She glared at him, her gray eyes as stormy as a weather front. "Why did you have to live in the middle of nowhere? What's wrong with civilization anyway?"

He shrugged, planting a booted foot against the inside of the door. "I like some space between me and my neighbor," he said, giving the door a good hard kick. It reluctantly creaked open, allowing him to escape. He reached into the back and plucked out the plastic bags of groceries. "You coming?"

She wasted several seconds shoving at the door on her side before giving it up as a lost cause. Wiggling out from behind the steering wheel, she tumbled headfirst through the open window. "How far is it to the ranch?"

"Not far. Fifteen, twenty miles. If we hustle, we'll be there by dinnertime." He tried not to chuckle at her expression. "I'm kidding, honey."

Relief blossomed across her expressive face. "It's not fifteen or twenty miles?"

"Oh, it's that far all right. But I expect we'll get a lift before we've hiked too many hours."

"Thank heaven."

He pointed his boots toward home and kicked them into gear. "And when we get there, I'm going to have to kill your son again."

"Hutch? What does he have to do with...?" She slowed to a stop, then turned around to glare at her car. "Oh, he didn't!"

"Odds on he did. Like teenagers on a first date, remember? Running out of gas is a classic."

With an exclamation of fury, she caught up with Ty, relieving him of some of the grocery bags. "You're not killing him," she announced in no uncertain terms.

"I'm not?"

"No. Because I'm gonna do it first."

"You know why he's pulling all these stunts, don't you?"

Cassidy blew out a sigh. "I know. But that doesn't mean he can keep setting us up like this. The bedroom incident was bad enough."

"Actually, I liked the power outage best." To his delight, a blush licked across her cheekbones. "That one came closest to working, don't you think? Of course, if we'd gone much further, one of us would have ended up with glass in our—"

"Talking to him hasn't helped," she hastened to cut in. "Perhaps if we simply ignored him? Once he sees it's not working, maybe he'll stop."

"And is it?"

"Is it what?"

"Is it not working?"

Cassidy quickened her pace. "No," she said emphatically. "It's not."

"Okay. Is it working now?"

Cassidy sagged to the floor of the saddle house, anger warring with her sense of the absurd. It had been close to a week since the incident with the car and they'd both hoped Hutch had given up on his little attempts to throw them together. Apparently, they were wrong. "I'm not so easily won over. You should know that."

"You'd think I'd have bought a clue by now," he muttered. He tried the knob to the small wooden building for the fiftieth time. It remained as solidly locked as the last time he'd attacked it. "Just what the hell did that kid think we were going to do in here anyway?"

"Talk?" she suggested. "Settle our differences?" Kiss? She played with the leather reins of a bridle dangling from a peg on the wall. The metal bit clunked overhead and she hastened to let go of the reins so the whole darn thing didn't fall on top of her. "Who can say with him? I haven't been able to follow his thought processes since he was four. I'm not likely to figure it out now that he's ten."

"What about Lonnie?" He skirted a pile of saddle blankets and ropes and joined her on the floor, dropping his Stetson onto his bent knee. "How did he handle Hutch?"

Her mouth thinned. "He handled his son the same way he handled everything."

"He ran."

"As fast and as far as his wallet would allow. Which was rarely too far since we were always broke."

"Did Hutch's brilliance intimidate him?"

"You might say that." She looked up at him. "Does it intimidate you?"

Ty tipped his head back against the wall, exposing the long, tanned line of his throat. "Hutch asked me that a number of times. Asked if it bothered me that he's so smart."

"And does it?"

"Not a lick. The only thing that bothers me is that he won't stop this nonsense. I thought you said ignoring it would help."

"I guess it's going to take a bit more ignoring."

"Or a few more chores to keep the boy too busy for mischief."

She gave a ladylike snort. "How long does it take to send me out here on a fool's errand and lock the door as soon as I step inside?"

"Wily little brat."

"He's certainly determined. Which makes me think..." She pulled her legs tight against her chest and rested her chin on her knees. Ty wouldn't like this next part. Heck, she didn't much like it herself. But she had to do something to put an end to this nonsense. "This is getting out of hand. It's time I made a serious effort to find a job and a new place to live."

"I thought you were going to stay here until after the Fiesta." His voice rumbled like a threatening volcano. "Staying here saves your having to pay rent and—"

"And gets Hutch's hopes up. It can't be good for him to spend so much time and energy throwing us together. Eventually, he's going to get frustrated. And angry."

Ty thrust a hand through his hair. "I think we were better off when we were ignoring the kid," he muttered. "Where the hell did all this talk of leaving come from?"

"You know it's always been in the works."

"Look…as long as we're here, we might as well put the time to good use. You keep saying you don't want to get involved again, but we already are."

"No—"

"The real question," he said, cutting her off, "is why you're so afraid to admit it. What harm will it do to confess having feelings for me?"

What harm? It would destroy her, that's what harm it'd do. When the passion died, as it was bound to, it would leave two strangers sitting in a room staring at each other. Perhaps there'd be other children by then, in addition to Hutch. More children to be made miserable when Ty got itchy feet or grew tired of seeing her face across the breakfast table each morning.

"It would cause too much pain when the relationship ended. And it would cause Hutch irreparable harm."

"Who says it's going to end?"

She leaped to her feet. "I do. And it will. It always does."

"That's the biggest load of bull—"

The door swung open and Lorenzo walked in. He took

one look at Ty and Cassidy and the expressions on their faces, did a quick one-eighty and hustled back outside.

"No, wait!"

Cassidy erupted toward the door. Along the way, she somehow managed to snarl her feet around a coil of rope and did a header straight for the floor. Ty caught her at the last possible instant. With a sigh, he tossed her over one shoulder and thrust the door open with the other.

"Sorry to be so clumsy," she told his back in a tiny, subdued voice.

"Clumsy? You?" Ty scooped his Stetson up off the floor and crushed it down on top of his head. "Hadn't noticed."

Ty stood on the porch and gazed out over his property with intense satisfaction. The past two and a half weeks had been the most interesting, frustrating and pleasurable he'd ever experienced. He'd become accustomed to having Cassidy nearby and—despite Hutch's antics—found the boy's inquisitive nature and undisguised enjoyment of their time together more fulfilling than he could have imagined. It fueled his soul.

Cassidy joined him on the porch, carrying a pair of steaming mugs. "It's chilly this morning. I thought you could use this to take the edge off."

"Thanks," he said, accepting the coffee. "But don't let this April cold snap fool you. It'll warm up soon enough. By this afternoon, it'll be on the high side of eighty-five."

"Wish I owned a swimsuit."

He grinned. "Not necessary for my benefit. I can make sure you have the pool area all to yourself and you can enjoy the fine art of skinny-dipping. I'll even give you a few pointers if you want."

"Gee, thanks."

He sidestepped her elbow and even salvaged most of his coffee. Sheer self-protection had taught him to stay fast on his feet these past weeks. With a few years under his belt or a decade or four, he'd have a black belt in Cassidydodging. He looked forward to it. "Don't forget about our Fiesta date," he thought to remind her. "We'll be leaving after lunch today and staying at the Menger for a couple of nights."

"I *had* forgotten," she admitted. He could tell something was bothering her by the way she gnawed on her lower lip. She finally turned the poor thing loose, leaving it plump and red and tempting as hell. "Is this really necessary? Can't we have our dates here instead of going to the expense of a hotel?"

"*Here* everyone's watching. *There* I'd have some privacy with you and wouldn't have to spend all day checking over my shoulder to see what stunt your son's about to pull." He didn't give her a chance to argue the point. "Give it up, Cassidy. Hutch bought the Fiesta special and that's what he's getting. The reservations are already made and Willie agreed to stay with the boy while we're gone. She'll arrive in time for lunch."

A frown formed between her brows warning that she hadn't given up the argument quite yet. "I don't know, Ty. I think we should talk about th—" She broke off, shading her eyes against the early morning sun. "Speaking of Hutch…what's he doing?"

Ty squinted. No question, the kid was up to no good. He was busily passing something from hand to hand as he slipped across the yard. As focused as he was on whatever he held, he hadn't noticed them yet. The boy stepped into a patch of sunlight and Ty caught a flash of yellow and red.

"Oh, sh—" He vaulted over the porch rail and loped toward Hutch, fighting for calm so he wouldn't frighten the boy.

Progress Report
Everything's proceeding right on schedule. Well…maybe

a little slower than on schedule. But I have high hopes. Just a few more experiments and I should have Mom and Ty right where I want them. Married and living happily ever after.

CHAPTER EIGHT

Experiment #8: Writing this one up ahead of time. Haven't finished with experiment seven yet, but this is it! Time is running out.
Goal: Mom needs to tell Ty everything. I don't think he knows she has a secret. Heck, she didn't even squeal to me about it. Not that she had to. I figured it out a long time ago. But I think she's afraid to tell Ty. Afraid he won't love her.
Procedure: Slip the letter that came for her today into her suitcase without her seeing.

"HEY, boy," Ty said quietly. "Nice snake."

Startled, Hutch looked up, a guilty expression creeping across his face. "I found it," he said, moving to hide the reptile behind him.

"Whoa there! Don't do that." Ty spoke more sharply than he'd intended and fought to moderate his voice. "Hutch, listen to me. I want you to put the snake down. Nice and easy."

"It's just a longnose." He held out his hands, allowing the snake to wriggle from one palm to the other. "I found it on a rock. I think it was after some sun cuz it's so cold this morning. Did you know that a longnose—"

"You can tell me all about it after you put it down," Ty interrupted with an edge of desperation.

Cassidy joined them, flinching back when she saw what Hutch was holding. "Oh, yuck! Why did you pick that up? You know how much I hate snakes."

Hutch's gaze skittered away. "Longnoses are really interesting, Mom. And pretty. I wanted to study him for a bit before letting him go.''

Ty glanced at the barn and saw a few of his wranglers headed toward them. If he couldn't convince the boy to get rid of the snake fast, all hell would break loose and someone would end up on the wrong side of a set of fangs. ''Hutch, listen carefully. If you don't put the snake down right this second, I'm going to start talking to your mom about caliper switches and eviction notices.''

It worked like a charm. Hutch tossed the snake aside. The closest wrangler saw it, let out a holler and began stomping his 13D Justin mulehides all over the fleeing reptile. With loud shouts, the others followed suit. Ty grabbed Cassidy and her son and hustled them from the scene of the massacre.

''Did you see what they did?'' Hutch demanded indignantly. ''Why didn't you make them stop?''

''Because if they hadn't killed it, I would have. That was no longnose, boy.''

''Not a—'' Hutch skittered to a halt, his face paling. ''That was a *coral* snake? I thought they were nocturnal.''

''They're poisonous, aren't they?'' Cassidy asked uneasily.

Hutch nodded vigorously. ''They're a member of the cobra family. And I actually picked one up. Cool! Heck, if it had bitten me, I'd probably be—''

Ty caught the boy in a bear hug, effectively muffling what he'd been about to say. ''*Sorry*. You'd have been real sorry. No harm done, Cassidy.'' She didn't look terribly convinced. He strove to sound casual and came close enough to pass muster if no one was listening too carefully. ''Hey, would you mind rustling up some more coffee? I'm afraid I spilled mine.''

''But the snake…?''

He risked a quick glance over his shoulder. ''Not likely to bother anyone any time soon.'' He made a mental note to make sure the few grisly pieces the wranglers had left behind were cleaned up before Cassidy returned. Fortunately, she didn't realize how bad the situation might have been if corals weren't so docile or if this particular one hadn't been fresh out of hibernation and too cold to kick up a fuss at being handled. If she'd known, she and the boy would undoubtedly be packed and gone within the hour. "Er...the coffee?"

"Okay," Cassidy said with a shrug. "I'll get it."

"Thanks." The instant she disappeared inside, Ty confronted Hutch. "You've really done it this time, boy. I'd talk fast, if I were you."

"I didn't know it was a coral. Honest."

"Kid, you know everything. How could you not know that? You must have heard the expression, 'Red and yellow, kill a fellow. Red and black, can't hurt Jack.' If the red and yellow bands are together, keep away from it. Got it?"

Hutch nodded. "Sorry, Ty. I didn't mean to scare you."

"Well, you did. If anything had happened to you..." Ty's jaw worked for a moment. "I would've had a hell of a time getting your mom to lay off the waterworks," he finished gruffly.

"Yeah. She would've been upset." Hutch hesitated. "Lonnie wouldn't have been, though."

Ty frowned. Where the hell had that come from? "Now why would you say such a thing?"

The boy made a face. "He didn't like me much. That's why he and Mom broke up, you know. Because of me."

"I thought it was over June July."

"April Mae." A brief grin flashed. "Naw. She wasn't the real reason. It was my fault."

What had prompted this? Something was sticking in the boy's craw and it had been there since they'd first met. Perhaps the time had come to get it sorted out. "Why do you think you're responsible for their breakup?" Ty asked conversationally.

Hutch kicked at a rock. It ricocheted across the yard and dinged the hubcap of Cassidy's rattletrap. "I heard him. It was the day Mom got my test scores back. The ones that told her how smart I was. I was only five, but I have a really good memory." He slanted Ty a quick look from beneath his lashes. "That's one of the things the tests discovered. About my memory. Well, anyway, I remember what Lonnie said and…"

"And?" Ty prompted.

Hutch lifted his shoulder in a casual sort of shrug. "I did tell you I was smart, didn't I?"

"Yeah, kid. You did."

"Scary smart. I told you that, right?"

Ty's gaze sharpened. "I believe you may have mentioned it."

"And it doesn't bother you? Not even a little?"

"Nope. In fact, it's one of the things I like best about you."

A flush crept into Hutch's cheeks. "You do? Really?"

"I wouldn't lie to you about something like that." He waited a beat, but the boy remained stubbornly silent. "Five years is a long time to have something eating at you. Might as well get it out into the open where we can have a look-see. What happened when the test results came in?"

"Oh, you know. Nothing much." Light, breezy, unconcerned…and lying through his teeth. "Mom put together this big party. She used some of her meat money to buy balloons and bake a cake, and hung up decorations and everything. I think she knew people would treat me differently when they found out I was a brainiac and this was her way of making me feel good about myself." Hutch made a production of adjusting his glasses. "When Da— Lonnie came home, I was in my room getting ready for our party. But I heard him. Mom told him all about how smart I was and he said…he said…"

"I gather he didn't like it," Ty offered gently.

Hutch gathered himself, his jaw clenched so tight it was a wonder his teeth didn't shatter. "He said I was a freak and he didn't want no part of me."

"Aw, Hutch…"

The story came tumbling out. "That's when Mom took his plate and glass from the cabinet and told him to get out and never come back. That stupid ol' April Mae was welcome to him since between the two of 'em they might come up with half a brain, which was all either of them were ever likely to need."

Go Cassidy, Ty thought fiercely. Damn, he wished he'd been there to cheer her on. With any luck at all, she'd have had all twenty-six inches swinging fast and furious. And her bastard of an ex would have tumbled out of there sorer, if not wiser. But that still left one small kid nursing a world of hurt. Slowly, Ty stooped until they met eye to eye. It took every ounce of self-possession to answer calmly. "Good thing you inherited your smarts from your mom's side of the family. Otherwise I suspect you'd have been as dumb as a rock."

Hutch blinked rapidly and offered a watery grin. "Guess so."

Ty nudged his Stetson to the back of his head and chose his words with care. "Hutch, this world is peopled by all sorts of folks. Some don't like anything that strikes them as different, and when they come across it they take fright and run. Or they say stupid things even if they don't mean them. I suspect your father is one of those types. Maybe someday he'll grow out of it and you'll be man enough then to let bygones be bygones."

"Maybe."

"But, kid, you can't color your world with Lonnie's crayons, if you know what I mean. Especially when he's only using one color. You can't allow his views of you to determine your views of yourself. Try not to let one mean, thoughtless remark scar you. It's not worth it. We're what we make of ourselves, not what others tell us we are."

"Then…" Hutch's chin trembled for an instant before he brought it under rigid control. "Then it's okay with you that I'm smart? It won't make you leave?"

"Not a chance," Ty said emphatically. "Your mom won't ever have to hand me my plate and glass because of you. Know why that is?"

Hutch's blue eyes clung, afraid and wary and desperate. "Not 'zactly."

Ty dropped heavy hands on the boy's skinny shoulders. "Because I love you as much as I would my own son. And I'm proud of you, kid. Proud and honored to have you as my friend."

Hutch's head dipped in acknowledgment. "Okay. That's good." He peeked shyly up at Ty. "You're not going to hug me or anything?"

Ty fought a grin. "I might."

"Well, okay." Hutch scuffed his feet in the dirt. "But just a quick one. And you better pound me on the back in case anybody's lookin'. That way, it's a guy thing and not like I'm a little kid and need a hug or anything."

Ty swept him up and held him as tightly as he dared. He didn't pound. Hospitalizing the kid probably wouldn't be wise. But he did tap a bit. Gently.

Very gently.

Tears filled Cassidy's eyes and she slipped silently off the porch, praying they didn't notice her. *He'd heard them.* All those years ago, Hutch had heard Lonnie's horrible, unforgivable words. For five years he'd sealed them up inside, allowing them to fester. And fester they had...until Ty had lanced the wound. Until he'd taken her son in his arms and given him the one thing she'd never been able to—a father's love and acceptance.

All this time, she'd been resisting any sort of involvement, despite the fact that it was an involvement she wanted every bit as much as Hutch. And why? It didn't take a lot of thought. She'd resisted because she feared being hurt. Because she was afraid to trust, afraid of the lies and halftruths that went along with the death of love. Afraid of being deserted and forced to pick up the shattered pieces

of their lives again. Afraid of living day to day on the edge
of survival with no hope or relief in sight.

Ty isn't Lonnie. Cassidy covered her face with her hands.
No, he wasn't. He was a man who'd offered love and acceptance from the first moment she'd catapulted into his
arms. He'd taken her in along with her son and done everything in his power to make them happy. And he'd keep
doing it, too. Because love wasn't a one-night stand for
him. It wasn't a few meaningless words of passion followed
by a quick tumble in the parking lot outside of a high
school gym. For Ty it was words backed up by deeds that
followed a consistent pattern—the same pattern that would
be repeated again tomorrow and the day after and the day
after that.

So, what the heck did she do now?

She began by wiping away her tears. Next she'd start
pointing her face toward the future instead of constantly
looking over her shoulder at the past. No wonder she
tripped so often! Then she'd trot on upstairs and pack for
her trip to San Antonio. And if Ty asked her to marry him
again, this time she'd say yes. This time, she'd allow love
to govern her actions instead of fear. This time, she'd open
her mouth and tell him what was in her heart, tell him that
she loved him with every fiber of her being and had from
the moment she'd accidently backhanded him.

Her days of running were over. This time, she'd grab her
happiness and hold on tight.

"What do you mean you've never been to the San Antonio
Fiesta?" Ty forged a path through the crowd lining the
River Walk. To Cassidy's amusement, people gave way
with nary a murmur. "Not even to see the River Parade?"

"I've never had the chance." Or the money.

He captured her hand and pulled her close. "Work, I
assume?"

"It's a good opportunity to earn some spare cash," she
admitted. In fact, she should be staffing one of the booths

or waitressing in one of the restaurants right now. People tended to tip well during Fiesta days.

Up ahead at La Villita, a mariachi band blocked the walkway and Ty slipped an arm around her shoulders, pulling her close so they could stand with a crowd of locals and tourists and enjoy the entertainment. Nearby, someone broke a *cascarone*. The colorfully decorated egg shattered, its confetti-filled contents catching on a fragrant breeze and scattering. The bright bits of paper caught in Cassidy's hair, mingling with the flower crown Ty had purchased for her, and she laughed. She couldn't remember when she'd last been so happy.

Ty leaned close so he could be heard above the music. "Hungry?"

"Starving."

He gestured toward a man striding through the crowd gnawing on a huge turkey leg. "Want one?"

She chuckled. "I'll pass, thanks. But I wouldn't say no to one of those fat tortillas."

"Ah. A gordita. You're on."

"So, how long until the floats go by?" She couldn't wait to see the parade of boats that drifted along the San Antonio River. She especially wanted to check out the beauty queens dressed in their magnificent Fiesta gowns—handsewn, beaded wonders, some with trains as long as twelve feet. "Do you think we'll be able to see? It's awfully crowded."

"I bought seats. We'll head over in a little while."

"And then what?"

An odd expression crept into his gaze. "We can party until dawn with the rest of San Antonio. Do some dancing. Drink margaritas. Or…"

"Or?" she prompted.

"We can go back to our rooms."

In the middle of the crowd, they were suddenly alone. The music and laughter and raucous chatter faded into silence and Cassidy filled her eyes with the man she loved.

He stood tall and solid, a rock in the middle of a surging river. She slipped closer, and for the first time, took the initiative. She wrapped her arms around him, lifted her face to his and sealed his mouth with the most determined kiss she'd ever pasted on a man. Around her, people cheered.

"You sure as hell pick your times, sweetheart," he growled. "I don't suppose you want to head back to the hotel now?"

"And miss the river parade?" she teased.

Carefully, he adjusted her flower crown, dislodging confetti as he combed the colored ribbons through her hair with his fingers. "I want this night to be special for you."

There wasn't a doubt in her mind. "It'll be special. For both of us."

"Then we'll wait. Tonight..." He smiled tenderly. "Tonight isn't going to be rushed."

No, Ty wasn't the type for a quickie in the back seat of a Chevy, she was willing to bet, not even as a teenager. "Okay. But kiss me again quick, so the wait won't seem so long."

He cupped her face. "My pleasure, sweetheart." When he'd done a thorough job of it, he wrapped an arm around her waist. "Come on. I reserved some seating near the Little Church."

By the time the parade was scheduled to start, he had a five-year-old girl in traditional Mexican dress perched on one knee, while her brother rode the other. Cassidy had managed to snag an infant from the exhausted mother seated next to her and spent almost as much of the next hour cooing at the baby as she did oohing at the entertainment. She hadn't realized how much she'd missed having a baby in her arms, maybe because she'd had so little time and energy to enjoy Hutch at this age. She peeked at Ty from beneath her lashes. Perhaps someday she'd come to the Fiesta holding their—

"Next year we'll bring Hutch," Ty said, interrupting her train of thought.

Startled, she could only stare. "Next year?"

"Yeah. I know he had to be in school this week, but this is too good for him to miss."

"Look!" shrieked the little girl. Her dusky curls spilled over Ty's hand where he held her securely on his knee. "The floats! They're coming."

Cassidy craned to see. Sure enough, the first of the platforms slowly motored down the river toward them. For the next hour, she cheered with the rest of the crowd, waving at the participants and clapping for the bands. But her favorite part was when the beauty queens passed by.

The crowd would shout, "Show us your shoes!" And to deafening cheers and applause, the women on the floats would lift the skirts of their hundred pound, beaded dresses to show off their running shoes. The incongruous sight always provoked a laugh. When the last float had disappeared around the river's bend and the last child had been dropped into his parent's waiting arms, Ty turned to Cassidy.

"Like it?"

"It was fantastic." She smiled up at him. "Thanks for tonight. I'm glad we stayed. I wouldn't have missed it for the world. Especially those fabulous gowns. How did everyone know they were wearing sneakers under their dresses?"

"The beauty queens always do, and it's our job to make them prove it." Nearby, a violin played softly and he reached for her hand. "How about a dance before we go?"

"Here?" She glanced around self-consciously. "Now?"

"Why not?"

He swung her into his arms and she drifted in a leisurely circle, content to be crazy so long as she did it with Ty. To her amusement, other couples joined them in the impromptu dance. With a murmur of pleasure, Cassidy closed her eyes and leaned into him. She fitted so beautifully, her head nestling at precisely the right angle between the crook of his shoulder and his chin. And for once her feet cooperated, allowing her to follow his movements with perfect coordination, responding to the subtle press of thigh and hip. Heaven help her, if they danced this well in bed, she'd be a thrilled—not to mention a thoroughly satisfied—woman.

At long last, the final note slipped into the crowd and vanished and an enthusiastic guitarist took over. With a murmur of regret, Cassidy eased from Ty's embrace. "I guess we should be starting back."

He cupped her face, his thumb stroking the sweeping ridge of her cheekbone. It was as though he needed to touch her and to keep on touching. She more than understood. Standing on tiptoes, she wrapped her arms around his neck. For a long moment, she gazed into his eyes. On the surface they seemed as green and untroubled as a mountain lake. But beneath she caught a glimpse of fiery determination.

He wanted her with a passion that hurt and had since they'd first met. He'd waited patiently while she'd circled, wary and distrustful, deciding whether or not to allow him close. Well, the wait was over. She'd made her decision. She kissed him then—a kiss of promise and faith, of love and commitment. He practically devoured her on the spot. In time, they drew apart and he stared down at her. She'd never seen him so serious before.

"We're getting this straightened out. Tonight."

She didn't pretend to misunderstand. "Yes."

It was all he needed to hear. He caught her hand in his and started off in the direction of their hotel. "You looked as excited during that parade as the little girl I was holding," he commented with amazing calm.

How could he remain so cool? She felt ready to shatter like a darned *cascarone*. "Did I?"

"I get the impression you didn't spend a lot of time being a kid, even when you were one."

"I had a pretty normal childhood." It was only later she got into trouble.

"You were raised by your aunt and uncle?"

"My parents died when I was four and they took me in," she confirmed. "We didn't always see eye to eye."

"Over Lonnie, for instance?"

"Oh, yeah. But they're kind people and they meant well. And as it turns out, they were right about him."

"How do you suppose they'd take to Texas?" he asked casually.

"Texas?" They'd reached the Menger. Across the street she caught a glimpse of the Alamo, a sight that never failed to move her. She hesitated beneath a streetlight and glanced up at Ty. "What are you suggesting?"

He shrugged, opening the door to the hotel. "I have that cabin standing around doing nothing. Now that the skunk stink's been cleared out, it would make a great little apartment for them. They could be as independent as they wanted or come on up to the main house for meals—"

"I can't imagine Gen. Robert E. Lee riding Traveller through the lobby here," she chattered uneasily. "I wonder if anyone gave him a hard time about it. They sure would today if somebody chose to ride a horse right through—"

"You're avoiding my question."

"Don't you think you have enough guests staying at the ranch?" she asked cautiously.

He didn't say anything until they'd reached the Victorian lobby in the older section of the hotel. "You want the truth?"

"Please."

He paused by an old Seth Thomas dial clock. "Honey, if forcing your aunt and uncle onto Texas soil at gunpoint would convince you to stay, I'd load up my shotgun and take off for Georgia tonight."

"I don't think that's necessary," she assured him, starting up the steps toward their rooms.

"I'm relieved to hear it, not that it changes how I feel or what I'm trying to do."

"But it's premature," she explained gently.

He waited until they'd reached their suite and unlocked

the door before saying anything further. "It won't be premature for long," he said, gesturing for her to precede him
into the room. "It's that time again."

She tried to hide her smile. "Time for what?"

"Time to ask you to marry me."

"Okay."

"So will you?"

"Yes."

He ran a hand along the back of his neck. "I mean, after
tonight, if that doesn't convince you—" His head jerked
up. "Did you say yes?"

"I think so." She wrinkled her nose. "Let's see. You
said, 'Time to ask you to marry me,' and I said, 'Okay'
and then you said, 'So will you?' and I said—" The rest
of her words were smothered beneath his mouth. "I
shouldn't have teased," she whispered. "I should have just
told you. I love you, Ty. I never thought I'd say those
words again, but I'd be lying if I pretended I felt otherwise."

His smile was infinitely gentle. "We did promise to be
honest with each other, didn't we, sweetheart?"

But she hadn't been. Not about everything. Would it
make a difference to him when he found out the truth?
Slowly, she slipped from his arms. "Wait here. There's
something I need to show you."

Crossing to her bedroom, she retrieved the envelope
Hutch had slipped into her suitcase. "This came for you,
Mom. Good luck!" he'd scrawled across the bottom. Why
it surprised her that he'd figured out her secret, she wasn't
sure. That darned kid knew everything. But her son still
loved her, she reminded herself fiercely, despite learning
the truth. And the fact that he'd put the envelope in her
suitcase suggested that he thought Ty would, too. In a few
minutes, she'd find out.

Ty was waiting for her when she returned, his long
strides eating up the sitting area as he paced. "What is it?

What's wrong?'' he demanded, thrusting a hand through his hair.

She'd worried him, she realized in dismay. "It's that promise we made. I told you I'd be honest and I haven't been.'' She stood before him, the most vulnerable she'd ever been in her entire life. The envelope crinkled in her hands. ''There's a couple more things on that Yellow Rose application form that we have to change.''

A tight smile touched his mouth. ''Just swear it's not the one that says 'sex' and I can live with it.''

''Oh, no problem,'' she managed to tease. ''I answered yes to that one.''

''Great.'' He started for her. ''That's all I needed to know.''

''No, it's not.'' She fended him off with her hand, backing him into a nearby chair. Then she crawled onto his lap and wrapped her arms around his neck.

A muscle jerked in his jaw. ''That bad, huh?''

''Maybe,'' she whispered against his chest.

''Let me guess. Your real name is Bonnie and Lonnie is actually Clyde and you used to work in the banking industry.''

''Nope.''

''You're a princess in disguise and we're going to have to move to some European capital and raise little dukes and duchesses.''

She shook her head with a husky laugh.

His throat constricted as he swallowed. ''You and Lonnie aren't really divorced,'' he whispered.

Is that what he thought? She gave him a reassuring hug. ''Trust me, we're divorced and I have the papers to prove it.''

''Well, honey, I'm fresh out of ideas. I don't suppose you want to tell me what the problem is?'' When she didn't answer, he gestured toward the envelope clutched in her hand. ''I assume it has something to do with that letter you're busy turning back into pulp. Tell me about it, sweet-heart. Tell me what's wrong.''

He was being so patient, so understanding. It wasn't fair to keep him in suspense like this. Not since it was only her pride at stake. ''I told you that when I left home with Lonnie, I was pregnant. But...'' She moistened her lips. ''But there's one more thing I may not have mentioned.''

''And what's that?''

''I...I also hadn't graduated from high school.''

He frowned. ''But you're twenty-nine. How could you not have...?'' A hint of color crawled across his cheek-bones. ''Never mind.''

She choked on a laugh. ''I didn't get held back, Ty. The truth is...'' She took a deep breath. ''I'm not twenty-nine, I'm twenty-six.'' She waited while that sank in.

It didn't take long. He shot up in the chair and her head cracked his chin. ''Damn! You were *sixteen* when you got pregnant with Hutch?''

''Well...almost.'' She struggled to escape his lap, but he wrapped his arms around her waist, refusing to let go. Giving up, she subsided against him. ''I'd just completed my sophomore year. Lonnie was a senior. We'd been dating for a couple of months and we went to the prom together.'' It was her turn to blush. ''Suffice it to say it was a mem-orable night and we didn't spend all of it dancing. Nor did we practice safe sex.'' Her mouth twisted. ''Talk about stupid kids.''

''Then you discovered you were pregnant?''

She nodded. ''It finally dawned on me at some point during the summer. Lonnie had already graduated and of-fered to take me with him when he left town. As soon as my aunt and uncle realized I was leaving—with or without their permission—they let us get married.''

''And then Lonnie deserted you the month before you gave birth?'' he questioned, disbelief evident in his gaze. ''He deserted a sixteen-year-old *child*.''

She shrugged, fighting to distance herself from the emotions those memories stirred. "He had a better job offer. Or so he said. He promised to send money."

"And did he?"

"Enough to get by." Barely. "He wasn't a total louse. But I wasn't in any position to work. Even if I hadn't been pregnant, it isn't easy for a sixteen-year-old to get full-time employment, as I soon found out. Not the sort that will pay for food and rent and baby-sitting fees. So, as soon as Hutch was born, I got a job by lying about my age. Since I looked older than sixteen and was so tall, I got away with it. Once I'd saved up enough money, I went after Lonnie."

"And that's how you lived for the next five years? Chasing Lonnie?"

She attempted a grin that fell short. "Sounds like a movie title, doesn't it?"

"What ended the chase?" He shook his head. "Never mind. I think I know."

Time for another confession. "I heard Hutch telling you about our breakup."

Ty shot her a telling look. "You should've given that man his walking plate and glass long before you did."

"I realize that now. But I was young and scared and it took a while to figure out that I could make it on my own, that I didn't need Lonnie."

"And now?" He flicked the envelope with his finger. "What's this?"

"This is the answer to a five-year dream." For a long time, she stared at the envelope with the Texas Education Agency's return address in the corner. Carefully, she ripped it open and unfolded the paper.

Progress Report

I'm back in school now. Mom enrolled me at this new place near Ty's ranch. But there's a biiiiig problem. SOMEBODY at my old school squealed about my science project and they want to see it pronto since the kids here are working on science projects, too. Guess it'll really hit the fan now, especially when they find out what I've been doing with all my reports.

CHAPTER NINE

Experiment #9: EXPERIMENTS TERMINATED!

CERTIFICATE of High School Equivalency, the diploma read. "Congratulations on the successful completion of the General Education Development Tests." Cassidy's five test scores were listed on a flap folded behind the thick piece of paper. Writing, social studies, science, literature and arts, and the most difficult for her, mathematics. She'd just squeaked by on that one. But she'd passed.

The embossed certificate tumbled from her hands and she buried her face against Ty's chest, soaking his shirt with tears. *She'd done it.* After five long, difficult years, she'd finally done it. She'd accomplished her last goal.

Ty held her tight and let her cry it out. "You're something special, you know that?" It took a moment to register the respect deepening his voice. "That's why you've been fighting me so hard, isn't it?"

She lifted her head, sniffing. "What do you mean?"

"I mean pride, independence and a good dollop of fear have been getting in our way."

"So that's been our problem, huh?" She gave a watery grin. "And here I thought it was my refusing to marry you."

"Well, that, too." He flicked a piece of confetti from her hair before dropping his hands to her shoulders and giving them a gentle squeeze. "My guess is that you've been working toward your GED ever since you got rid of Lonnie." It wasn't really a question. "You wanted to prove you could."

"I decided I had to take charge of my life," she confirmed. "I was twenty-one, working a dead-end job, had a five-year-old genius to support and was about to be divorced. That's not the sort of life I'd planned for myself growing up."

"So you decided what you wanted out of life and went after it." He regarded her with steady, understanding eyes. "Sounds rather overwhelming."

"It was, except…" A look of determination crept across her face. "Except I suddenly realized I was perfectly capable of taking care of myself and my son. Heck, I'd been doing it those five years I'd been chasing after Lonnie. That's when I knew what I had to do. I had to go back to school and earn my diploma so I could get a decent job, and I had to mend fences with Aunt Esther and Uncle Ben."

He shook his head in wry amusement. "But then I came into your life and disrupted all your fine plans. What did you think I was trying to do, Cassidy? Steal your independence?" He cupped her face, admiring the strength of character revealed in every single beautiful line, even though her stubbornness caused him unending frustration. "Don't you understand? I'm not trying to steal anything or hurt you in any way. I'm just trying to make you happy."

"Happy?" Her laugh stirred the air between them, warm and sweet and startled. "That's the first time anyone's ever offered me that."

"I'm sorry to hear it. Because there's not a person on this planet more deserving of happiness than you. All you have to do is reach for it."

She closed her eyes and he feathered a kiss across the lids. "I'm so afraid," she whispered, shivering beneath the tender caress.

"I know you are. You don't like risk and I understand why." His hands slipped deep into her hair. "It's time to take a chance, sweetheart. You're going to have to trust me. What's worse…you're also going to have to trust yourself. Granted, you've made some bad choices in your life. But I swear, this isn't one of them.''

"I just have to believe that we're not making a mistake, huh?'' A shaky laugh escaped her. ''You don't ask much, do you?''

"Nah.'' His precious voice rumbled over her. ''Not me.''

"But don't you see? I haven't been fighting for my own sake. If something goes wrong with our relationship, Hutch—''

"Hutch needs a father,'' Ty interrupted. ''If I was a man who played fair, I wouldn't use that card. But the two of you have become too important to me. You've become a part of my life and I can't imagine you not in it. When I walk into the house, I find myself listening for you or looking around for a noisy squirt with bright yellow hair and mischief in his eyes. I always thought I had a home. Now I know how wrong I was. It's you and Hutch who've turned it into a home.''

By the time he ground to a halt, she was weeping again. "I love you, Ty. I do.''

"And I love you. Would poetry help convince you? How's this? You're the dawn after a long, bad night. You're the rain after the endless drought that's been my life. Don't you get it, sweetheart? You and Hutch are my future. And I'm yours.''

"How can you be so sure?'' she demanded. ''How can you be certain it's not going to end?'' *Like Lonnie.* The unspoken words hung between them.

"I can be sure because, unlike the voices you hear, my voices have no doubts and they don't give bad advice.'' He softened his reply with a smile. ''The first time I kissed you, remember? I knew. And so did you. The difference is...while it made me more determined to pursue a relationship, it frightened you off.''

The fight drained out of her. ''You're right. It did.''

"And you've been running scared ever since.''

She seemed to gather herself as though preparing to leap some insurmountable hurdle. "I'm not running now."

It was all the invitation he was going to get...and all he needed. He lowered his head and captured the sweetness of her sigh. Tasted it, savored it. Drowned in it. She wrapped her arms around his neck. She even did it without half killing him in the process. Not that he'd have cared if she had. What was a broken nose compared to the pleasure of her in his arms?

She was long and lanky and lush and fitted him better than any woman he'd ever taken to bed. He swung her around so she straddled him, groaning at the feel of her so tight against him. Her lips parted, allowing him greater access, and he surged inward. At the same time, he tugged at the drawstring that held her peasant blouse in place. Ripe, firm breasts tumbled into his hands. She groaned, wriggling closer.

"Wait a sec." It almost killed him to stop now, but somehow he found the strength of will. "Maybe we should have discussed this before."

Cassidy stared at him, dazed. "Discussed what?"

"Your intentions."

"Good gravy, Ty." She buried her face in his shoulder with a breathless laugh. "Your timing stinks, you know that? I'm sitting half-naked on your lap. In fact, if we were any closer, I'd be pregnant again. And you're asking me what my intentions are? I'd have thought that was obvious."

"Sorry, sweetheart. But I don't want any morning-after regrets. In a few minutes, I'm tossing you on that bed over there and we're gonna make sweet love until I'm too exhausted to move or until you knock me unconscious, whichever comes first."

A shiver fluttered through her. "Sounds good to me."

"Yeah, well...you mentioned getting pregnant. Don't you think we should discuss that?"

"I'm prepared this time. I...I visited a drugstore earlier

and..." She shrugged. "I figured one of us should take precautions."

His breath escaped in a ragged laugh. "Looks like we were both on top of it. I visited that drugstore, too." Okay, one problem out of the way, one to go. "But I gotta tell you, honey, I'm not taking you to bed until I have a commitment. You can't seduce me tonight and then toss me aside tomorrow."

She feathered a kiss across his mouth. "What if I promised to respect you in the morning?" she teased. "Would that be good enough?"

"Nope. I'm an old-fashioned sort of guy. It's a wedding ring or nothing."

"Okay, you win." She slipped off his lap, drawing her blouse closed over her breasts. Sinking to her knees in front of him, she took his hand in hers. "Will you do me the honor of marrying me, Mr. Merrick? I promise to love and care for you all the rest of my days."

About damned time. "Lady, I thought you'd never ask. I do. I will. And my pleasure." With a growl of satisfaction, he plucked her off the floor and into his arms. Three quick strides brought them to the edge of the bed. Sweeping the comforter off the mattress, he dropped his bride-to-be on the soft white sheets. Her blouse parted, slipping off her shoulders and drooping low over her breasts. The hem of her skirt rode high on her thighs, flirting with the plain cotton of her underpants. She had the longest legs he'd ever seen—the ankles narrow, the calves trim—legs perfectly fashioned to wrap around a man and never let go.

"This would probably be a good time to pick a fight with you," she said.

His brows drew together. "Come again?"

She sat up, wrapping her arms around her knees. "Don't you remember how you promised to end any further disagreements?"

The memory clicked in place and he rapidly thumbed buttons through buttonholes. "I believe it had something to do with stripping off my clothes until you gave in.'' He tossed his shirt to the floor, chuckling at her sigh of satisfaction. ''You should have seen your expression when I changed outside of Freddie's.''

A faint blush touched her cheeks. ''I figured you did it on purpose so you could show off all those ripples.''

''Sorry to disappoint you. I did it because you'd practically ripped the shirt off my back while we were in that café.'' He reclined on the bed next to her, playing with the dangling drawstrings of her blouse. ''I know it was an accident, but—''

''You think so, huh?'' Her smile gave him an idea of what Adam had faced in the Garden of Eden.

He cocked an eyebrow. ''Are you saying it wasn't?''

She shrugged, the rolling movement giving him a glimpse of heaven. ''You ended up with your shirt off, didn't you?''

''And you, sweet liar, ended up with a blush that went from the top of your head all the way down to your tippytoes.'' He tugged at her drawstring, fascinated by the slow downward slide of her blouse. ''Not that that stopped you from staring.''

''Ty...'' Her throat moved convulsively. ''I've never done this before with anyone except Lonnie.''

''I know, and I won't rush you.'' And he didn't. His movements were slow and nonthreatening, clothes sliding first from her body, then from his own. ''What's going to happen tonight won't be anything like what you shared with him.''

She closed her eyes, praying he was right. ''Promise?''

''I promise.'' He gathered her close. ''Honesty and trust, remember?''

Her laughter sounded strained. ''It must have slipped my mind.''

''That's okay. It hasn't slipped mine.'' He smiled down at her. ''Just focus on the ripples and you'll do fine.''

She reached for him, reassured by his solid strength. "There are so many it might take me a while."

"That's what I'm counting on."

Then the long night crept across the room, offering them shadows in which to conceal their intimate whispers and contain their husky laughter. Only the moon dared eavesdrop on the lovers, playing across soft, feminine curves and hard, bronzed angles and turning their bed into a silvered nest. And in those twilight hours, Ty won himself a bride, won her with a love so deep and so profound there was no more room for fear or doubt or independence. Their joining mated them. Completed them. Made them whole.

And Cassidy... That night, Cassidy finally accepted the truth.

Ty really wasn't Lonnie.

The phone rang, dragging Ty from a sound sleep. He rolled over with a groan, knocking the receiver off the hook. By the time he'd found it, he'd succeeded in waking Cassidy.

"What's wrong?" she murmured. "Who is it?"

"I'll tell you in a minute. 'Lo?"

"That Cassidy's voice I'm hearing?" Willie's voice boomed across the line.

"None of your business, old gal."

She chuckled. "I'll take that as a yes. Good on ya, boy. Listen, sorry to interrupt your Fiesta fun, but I'm afraid you'll have to cut it short."

That didn't sound good. Ty slanted a glance in Cassidy's direction. So far, she displayed only mild curiosity. For his own physical well-being, he'd prefer she stay nice and relaxed. "So what's up?"

"The school called."

"And...?" A flailing elbow caught him in the ribs and he hastened to moderate his tone. "Oh, really? Why?"

"Oh, shoot. He's fine, he's fine. Sorry. I worried you for a minute there, didn't I?"

"Just for a minute."

"There's nothing wrong with the boy. Not physically."
Laughter drifted across the line. "At least not yet. But he's
gotten the teachers in an uproar over something. They've
asked Cassidy to come to the school right away."

"This can't wait until tomorrow?"

"Apparently not. And Ty…"

"Yeah?"

"They want you there, too."

Uh-oh. "*Me*? What the hell for?" Cassidy's elbows
started flailing again and he threw an arm around her, plas-
tering her to his side. Unfortunately, her knees took up
where her elbows had left off.

"You're asking me that? You know the boy. What trouble do you think he's gotten himself into this time?"

The possibilities were endless. "We'll be there in a couple of hours," he said, and hung up.

Now he had a choice. He could either escape the bed
and tell her the news from a safe distance, or he could
confine her tightly enough to escape serious injury. After
the night they'd shared, he knew which he'd choose. He
rolled over on top of her, wrapping himself around the most
delicious piece of femininity he'd ever had the pleasure of
holding.

"I've got something to tell you.…" he began.

"I just don't understand," Cassidy fussed. "He's been
there less than a week. What could he have done in just a
couple of days?"

Wisely, Ty kept his opinion to himself. "Beats me"
seemed a safe response.

"I mean, he's only ten. How bad can it be?"

Considering how well his answer had worked last time,
he decided to try it again. "Beats me," he repeated.

"And they want to see you, too?"

"Beats me."

"What?"

"Oh. I mean, yeah, they want to see me, too."

"Why?"

He shrugged. "I assume we'll find out when we get there."

The minute they stepped into the office, they were ushered into a conference room. From the amount of gawking going on, Ty had a *really* bad feeling about what had happened. A few minutes later, the principal walked in with a woman he introduced as Mrs. Lopez, the seventh-grade science teacher.

"Thank you for coming so promptly," the principal said, offering his hand first to Cassidy and then to Ty. "I'm Kyle Peters."

"Has Hutch done something wrong?" Cassidy burst out, clearly unable to contain herself a minute longer. The principal and Mrs. Lopez exchanged troubled glances and she groaned. "I know that look. What is it this time? Did he blow up the lab? I'll replace the equipment, I promise. It's just that he's so smart and so curious—"

"The lab's fine, Ms. Lonigan," Mrs. Lopez hastened to assure her.

"And...uh...all the school's computers work? They don't do anything...odd?"

Alarmed, they stared at Cassidy. "Not as far as we're aware."

"Oh, okay, then." She beamed in relief. "Well. I guess that just leaves the snake."

The principal's hands tightened around the folder he was holding. "What snake is that?"

"That coral snake he picked up the other day. I can explain. You see—"

"Er, no." Mr. Peters blanched. "This has nothing to do with snakes."

"Honey, why don't you let them tell us what the problem is instead of scaring these nice people by guessing?" Ty suggested.

"Oh. All right. But if it's about that time he turned everyone blue—"

"*Cassidy!*"

With a weak smile, she subsided. "Sorry."

"It's about his science project," Mrs. Lopez hastened to say. "His former school told us he'd been assigned one, and since it fitted in with our current curriculum, I asked to see it."

Cassidy looked blank. "A science project? That's *it?*" She offered a huge, relieved grin. "What's he want to do this year? Gene splicing? Level five viruses? Cure cancer?"

"Not exactly." Mr. Peters frowned. "I've sent someone to bring Hutch to the office so we can discuss this with him, as well. But first I thought we'd fill you in. I don't quite know how to say this other than to come right out and tell you. He wants to marry you off to Mr. Merrick. It's a…a love experiment, I guess you'd call it."

Ty cursed beneath his breath. Of course. That explained all the cute little stunts. Love…logic-style. "I'm gonna kill that kid."

"I gather you don't approve," Mr. Peters said.

"Actually, I do approve." What he didn't approve of were the looks they were leveling Cassidy's way. Like she'd done something wrong raising the boy.

"Perhaps you don't realize the full scope of what he's attempted," Mrs. Lopez offered. She flipped open the folder in front of her. "According to his notes, he went to Yellow Rose Matchmakers with the express purpose of finding a—"

"A father," Ty interrupted. "Yes, I know. I have from the beginning. My grandmother and I own the Yellow Rose. I was there when Hutch showed up."

Mr. Peters lifted an eyebrow. "And you approve of this sort of manipulation?"

Ty leaned across the table so they could get a clear look at his expression. He wanted to be certain they saw just how serious he was. "I'm all for anything that will get Hutch's mother to marry me. Hell, if pasting wings on cows and tying rockets to their backsides so they could be shot over the moon would get Cassidy to marry me, I'd be the first one in the pasture with a bucket of glue."

In desperation, they turned to Cassidy. "You realize Hutch set everything up? He caused you to lose your apartment. He disabled your car battery so you'd be at Mr. Merrick's mercy. He…" Mrs. Lopez blushed. "He disconnected your bed rails."

Cassidy waved a hand through the air. Ty ducked. Mrs. Lopez flinched backward. Mr. Peters wasn't so quick or so lucky. "Oh, sorry. I didn't mean to hit you. You see, I have this false body image and my arms are three inches—"

"Sweetheart? Let's stick to the bed rails."

"Oh, right. Hutch wanted Ty to come to my rescue. Like a knight in shining armor-type thing."

"If you say so," Mr. Peters said dubiously.

"Hey! He's only ten years old. He wasn't thinking about…he wasn't trying to…" It was Cassidy's turn to blush. "It wasn't a bed thing. It was a rescue mission."

"Let's start with the apartment," Mrs. Lopez suggested. "He caused you to get evicted. Doesn't that concern you in the least?"

"See, you're wrong there. We were evicted because of Miz Mopsey."

"That's the dog."

"That's right." Cassidy tilted her head to one side, the beginnings of a frown puckering her brow. "How did you know?"

Mrs. Lopez tapped her notes. "It's here under Plan B." She slipped a pair of glasses on the tip of her nose. "I quote, 'Walk Miz Mopsey past Mrs. Walters's door and make a racket. Maybe she'll notice for once.'" The teacher glanced up. "Unfortunately for you, she did."

"Look…is all this necessary?" Ty demanded. "If Cassidy had gone in to talk to the woman, she'd have found out they didn't have to move that night. Doris would have given them time to find a new place."

"How do you know *that*?" Cassidy asked, her frown

deepening. "Come to think of it, how do you know her first name?"

He shrugged uneasily, realizing too late that he'd given away more than he should have. "I didn't think it was proper that she throw you out in the middle of the night. So I talked to her about it when I went to pick up your car."

"Ah, yes. The car." Mrs. Lopez shuffled some papers. "It didn't work because of a burned out... Here it is. A caliper switch."

"A caliper switch? No such thing," Mr. Peters interjected.

Ty nodded. "Yeah, I know. It was the battery cables."

Cassidy rounded on him, catching him in the ribs. "You knew? You knew and didn't say anything?"

Damn. "You didn't want my help, remember?" he retorted defensively, clutching his side. "I offered and you said hell no, let the kid do it. If you'd bothered to ask, I'd have told you what was wrong with the rattletrap."

"I did not say hell." She turned to address the school officials. "I did not say hell. I don't swear."

"Yeah, well, you didn't say help, either. And since you didn't, I didn't."

She swiveled again; Ty recoiled again. "Because you wanted to take me home with you. So you lied."

"That's right. No! That's—"

"Moving along..." Mr. Peters interrupted. "Shall we talk about the skunk that got into the cabin?"

"Shall we not?" Ty suggested hopefully.

Cassidy folded her arms across her chest, the first safe move she'd made since they'd gotten there. "Don't try to tell me Hutch is responsible for that, because I won't believe you. He couldn't have found a skunk and then lured him into our cabin in the little bit of time we were at Ty's."

"Knowing your boy, I'm not so sure," the principal observed tartly. "But, in this case, you're right. That's not what he did."

"I didn't think so."

"Instead, he set off some chemicals that smelled like a skunk."

"They didn't do a bit of harm," Ty insisted. "And I had a long talk with him about it and made him scrub the cabin from top to bottom. You'll notice he didn't try anything like that again."

"You *what*?" Cassidy erupted from the chair, practically knocking him to the floor.

He rubbed his sore shoulder. Jeez! That's what he got for defending her son. Next time, the kid could take the heat all by his lonesome. "What? What did I do?"

"You knew about all these things he did and never told me?"

Ty climbed to his feet. "You caught on eventually! Remember when we ran out of gas? I told you then it was Hutch and you said we should ignore him."

Hurt turned her eyes to pewter. "I'm his mother. You should have let me know what he was up to from the start."

"Why? So you'd have an excuse to leave? Damn it, Cassidy. I'd just gotten you there. If I'd ratted on the kid, you'd be in Georgia right now."

"You promised to be honest with me!"

"I think I see what happened," Mr. Peters said. "Hutch contrived all these incidents and Mr. Merrick encouraged him."

"That is *not* what happened." Ty glared at the principal. "You're missing the point here. This ten-year-old boy is desperate for a father. And so, in his own inimitable fashion, he decided to do something about it. Because of the way his mind works, he went about it in a very methodical manner, using logic and intelligence to try to—"

"Manipulate people. Mr. Merrick, I appreciate that you've put up with all this to help out your grandmother and protect your joint business interests, but you must agree it's not appropriate."

Cassidy slowly sank into her chair. "Excuse me? What did you say?"

"I am *not* doing this for my grandmother's sake," Ty interrupted in hardened tones. "I told you why I was doing this. Winged cows with rockets on their butts, remember?"

"Are you sure? With all the bad publicity Yellow Rose Matchmakers has received recently, I can understand why you'd be so accommodating to Ms. Lonigan and her son. I suspect you can't afford any more problems."

"Oh, no," Cassidy whispered.

Mr. Peters shot her a pitying glance. "There's more."

Ty's hands clenched. How he wished he could wrap them around the principal's throat. Everything he'd done could be explained. Though the way the school officials were doing the explaining, it would like as not break Cassidy's heart, not to mention his arms and legs. "I think we've heard all we need to."

"I'm afraid you haven't. Hutch told us about the reporters who were at Yellow Rose when he first showed up. They've been chronicling his adventures. Were you aware he's been sending them progress reports?"

"No," Ty bit out, "I wasn't."

"Wait a minute!" Cassidy's hands started fluttering again—always a bad sign. He shifted a few inches to the left. Mr. Peters and Mrs. Lopez followed suit. "I want to know what you're talking about. What bad publicity? What has any of this got to do with the Yellow Rose?"

Ty gave it one last shot. "I'll tell you later."

"No, you'll tell me right now."

"Okay, fine. It's no big deal. A magazine reporter discovered that one of my grandmother's employees—Wanda—wasn't using the computer to make her matches." He fought to control his fury—with limited success. "It may interest you to know that her success rate outstripped the machines. But because we're billed as a computer dating service, certain individuals suggested fraud was involved. When it all hit the fan, my grandmother ran every last questionable profile through the computer, and whad-daya know? The computer confirmed Wanda's matches. End of story.''

"Well, not quite," Mrs. Lopez retorted. "You fail to mention the follow-up article and its importance to Yellow Rose's future. You need them to give you a positive write-up, don't you?"

For the first time since he'd known Cassidy, Ty saw her look completely devastated. Her arms folded around her waist like a drooping flower blossom. Worst of all, she didn't move. Not a twitch, not a fidget, not a knee or elbow or finger out of place.

"That's why you were so annoyed when the computer matched us," she whispered. "With the reporters watching, you didn't have any choice but to date me."

Ty thrust a hand through his hair. "Yeah, okay. You're right. I had no choice at that point. But then something happened and you know it."

She bowed her head. "Hutch started manipulating us."

"No, damn it all!" he roared. "We kissed. Remember that kiss? I sure do. It had one hell of an impact on me, even if it didn't on you."

"Mr. Merrick, please! This is a school."

He fought his frustration. "Where's the kid? Get him now. We're leaving before you screw up my life any fur-ther."

"Yes, please," Cassidy agreed.

"Will wonders never cease?" he muttered. "She finally agrees with me about something. I knew that ninety-nine percent had to kick in eventually."

"I do agree, Ty. Leaving is a good idea. Actually, it's an excellent idea." A travesty of a smile crept across her mouth. "I'm sorry about the science project, Mrs. Lopez. I'll have Hutch come up with a new one during our move to Georgia."

She said it so sweetly. So brightly. In fact, everything about her was bright. The hot blush glowing across the full sweep of her cheekbones. Her perky, Southern-syrup voice. The tremulous smile pasted on the mouth he'd kissed with such passion a few short hours ago. But brightest of all were her tear-laden eyes. It took every ounce of self-restraint to keep from sweeping her into his arms and carrying her out of the place.

"You are *not* moving back to Georgia," he informed her through gritted teeth. "We're engaged, in case you've forgotten."

"I hardly think this is the place to discuss—"

"You're right." He turned to the principal again. "But just so you know…just so there's not a single, solitary question in your minds, *I* not only approve of Hutch's experiment, I'm proud of him." He climbed to his feet, sweeping Cassidy up with him. "He wanted a father. What could be a more worthy goal than that? In this crazy world, if that isn't the smartest, most practical scientific endeavor a boy could work toward, I don't know what is. And I'll tell you something else. I'm gonna make sure his experiment succeeds." He slammed his Stetson down on his head. "In fact, I'm gonna make sure he gets a friggin' A+ on it."

If Cassidy had clipped him with a single finger, elbow or knee in protest, he'd have tossed her over his shoulder and been done with it. Perhaps she didn't because she was expending all her energy in keeping her tears from falling. He grimaced. For a woman who never cried, she sure as hell was the cryingest female he'd ever come across.

Just as they exited the conference room, Hutch scurried up. He took one look at their faces and slipped his arms through the straps of his backpack. "I guess we're going, huh?"

"Oh, yeah. We're going." He caught Mr. Peters's eye. "But we'll be back."

Hutch approached the principal and held out a large envelope. "Here."

"What's this?" Mr. Peters asked.

"It's my other science project. You and Mrs. Lopez should like it okay. It's about irrigation and erosion and how to make sure we have enough water to grow all the food we need. It's not the one I wanted to do because right now I don't care about anything but my mom." His mouth curved downward. "I was just trying to make her happy, you know. And maybe get a dad."

"But, Hutch," Mrs. Lopez protested, "someone could have been hurt. What about your seventh experiment? I gather you were going to put that snake in your mother's room. I realize you weren't aware it was a coral, but—"

"Hutch?" Ty growled.

"I wasn't! Honest. I was really just looking at it. Snakes scare Mom. I wouldn't have taken it anywhere near her. I even tried to hide it behind my back until Ty threw a fit."

"Then what was your seventh experiment?" the teacher asked.

Hutch shrugged, a hint of color brightening his cheeks. "I was going to put some of Mom's bubble bath in the pool. I thought it would be romantic."

Mrs. Lopez released a long, drawn-out sigh. "Give us a day to discuss this a little further, Mr. Merrick. There may be some value to what you've said."

A lot of value, he almost retorted, before deciding discretion might be a wiser course of action at the moment. "Thanks. I appreciate it."

Wrapping his arms around Cassidy and Hutch, he ushered them from the building. The minute they hit the parking lot, she pulled free. "Please take us to the nearest motel, if you'd be so kind."

Judging by her expression, he was in it up to his boot tops. "No, I won't be so kind. You've got to listen to me, Cassidy—"

"I most certainly do not. You lied to me."

"I never lied. I didn't tell you what Hutch was up to, but that's because I really *didn't* know what Hutch was up to." He nudged the boy. "Tell her, kid."

"I never told Ty I was working on a science experiment. Honest. He figured out I wanted a dad, but he thought all the pranks were from me being smart."

"Scary smart," Ty added. Cassidy kept walking and he began to feel a hint of desperation. "Granted, I should have told you about the apartment. And the car. And the skunk. I admit that. But I knew the kid didn't mean any harm and it gave me the perfect opportunity to court you."

That slowed her down. "Court me?"

"It's an old-fashioned word, I agree. But it sure fits what I was hoping to do."

"That doesn't change the fact that you were trying to protect your business interests by dating me."

"Damn it, woman. That tears it. There's only one way to win an argument with you." He ripped open his shirt, buttons pinging in every direction. He tore it off his shoulders, balled it up and flung it onto the concrete parking lot. "I did not, I repeat, did *not* date you for my grandmother's sake or for the sake of the agency."

Cassidy rounded on him, wide-eyed. "Ty! What are you doing? Stop that!"

"The hell I will. I'm not stopping until you quit arguing and say you love me. Now where was I? Oh, yeah. I am not marrying you to save Willie's business." He did the unthinkable next, something a cowboy would never do. He yanked off his Stetson and threw it on the ground. "And I'm sure as hell not marrying you because of any magazine article."

She held up her hands. If she'd been any closer, she'd have coldcocked him silly. "All right, all right. I believe you!"

"Sorry, honey. I didn't catch what you said." He hopped up and down on one foot, grabbed the heel of his size fifteens and started yanking. "Don't just stand there. Help me, boy."

Hutch stared at him as though he'd lost his mind. "You want me to pull off your boot?"

"If it wouldn't be too much trouble." Still hopping, he said, "I'm in love with you, you fool woman. I want to marry you because I'm crazy about you, not because of any scientific experiments or because of bad publicity." He planted a sock-covered foot on the ground and held out his other foot to Hutch. "Don't dawdle. Toss that one aside and start on this'un. And then go get in the truck. It might get downright embarrassing from here."

Hutch didn't wait to hear more. The minute he'd yanked Ty's boot free, he scurried across the parking lot and disappeared from sight.

"Okay, woman. We're getting down to the serious stuff now." This better work or he'd light up all of San Antonio with his blush. "Do you believe me or do I bare my assets to the world?"

"Stop it!" Cassidy begged. "I give up. I believe you."

"Well, that's something." He stood in his stocking feet, fists planted on his hips, and faced her down. "But it's still not good enough."

"What else do you want me to say?"

"Not much." He dropped his hand to his belt buckle. "How about, I believe you. I know you wouldn't do anything as unscrupulous as those people said. How about, I love you, Ty. I've always loved you. And I'd trust you with my life. That might make a good start." She flew into his arms and he staggered under the impact. His poor ripples were going to be one mass of bruises by morning. But it would be worth it.

"I love you, Ty. I've always loved you. And I do trust you, not just with my life, but with my son's, too."

"And when are you going to marry me?"

"Right away. As soon as we can get a license."

"And where are you going to live?"

"Wherever you want." She peeked up at him. "But I'm hoping it's on the prettiest ranch in all of Texas."

He lowered his head and branded her with a kiss. He'd have done more, but he had enough sanity left to remember where they were. "Okay, then. Now that you've made me look like a total idiot in front of all Hutch's schoolmates, you can help me pick up my clothes."

She bent down and retrieved his hat, dusting off the brim. "I would have given in sooner, you know."

He scowled. "You would have?"

"Yeah." She grinned. "But I wanted to see how far you'd go."

He slapped his Stetson on top of his head and gave her a wink. "Honey, for you I'd have gone all the way."

It was during the brief drive back to the ranch that Cassidy finally realized the truth. She was going home. A home where she belonged. Where people were waiting for her and would welcome her with open arms.

When they arrived, Willie stood in the yard. Beside her hovered a nervous looking couple. Cassidy inhaled sharply. "Aunt Esther!"

"And your uncle Ben." Ty parked the truck and turned off the engine. He shot her an apologetic shrug. "I guess this is one more thing I should've come clean about. I invited them for a surprise visit. Where it goes from here is up to the three of you. But that cabin's all theirs if you want."

She threw her arms around Ty's neck—only nicking his nose a little bit—and kissed him. Oh, how she loved him. How could she ever have doubted it? She glanced across the yard at the couple who'd raised her, more apprehensive than she cared to admit.

"Go on," Ty encouraged her. "They're as scared spitless as you."

Slowly, Cassidy left the haven of the truck and approached her aunt and uncle. There was a momentary hesitation and then the three were hugging and crying and talking all at once. They were also tripping over each other and knocking elbows a bunch, which explained a lot about Cassidy. Apparently, false body images ran in the family.

At long last, she pulled free. Turning, she gestured to Hutch.

He held back, pointing at the bushes on either side of the porch steps. "Mom, look! Your roses are covered in buds."

She stared in disbelief. They were covered and covered some more. She'd never seen so many blossoms. But then, why should she be surprised? "Seems like they've found the perfect home to put down roots, just like us." She ushered her son forward. "Come and meet your relatives, sweetpea. And then I want you to introduce them to your new dad." Her gaze met Ty's. "I know they're going to love him as much as we do."

EPILOGUE

"Okay, ladies, stick out your glasses and I'll pour the champagne. No, no, Wanda. Sit and relax," Willie insisted, waiting until the seventy-six-year-old woman had stopped fluttering long enough to find a chair. That's what she got for hiring an escaped fairy godmother from a Disney flick. The woman couldn't move without fluttering. If she wasn't so good at her job... "And, Maria, if you answer the phone again, I'll have one of your relatives tie you to that chair."

She waited until Maria had finished rapping out instructions in Spanish to one of said relatives and was sipping champagne before whipping out the magazine article. "Wait until you hear this update...." She took a quick swallow from her glass and settled into her chair. Plucking a yellow rose from a nearby vase, she waved it at them for emphasis as she began.

"'*Ten-year-old boy uses Yellow Rose Matchmakers and science to snag himself a dad,*'" she read. "That's the headline. Then it says, 'Yellow Rose Matchmakers made Hutch Lonigan quite a deal. For just nine dollars and change they gave him the best date ever...a date with destiny. After filling out an application for his mother, Cassidy Lonigan, Yellow Rose's computer spat out the perfect father for young Hutch—the grandson of owner, Willie Eden. But it took a few scientific experiments to convince his mother that Ty Merrick was the perfect husband for her. "I got an A+ on the project at school," Hutch said proudly. "But best of all, I got a dad." It looks like the Yellow Rose's computer matches are back on track!'"

Willie tossed the magazine aside with a sigh and lifted her glass. "Cheers, ladies. I suspect business is going to be booming. Oh! And before I forget, you were right, Wanda. I reran Cassidy's application one last time with her correct age and darned if it didn't come up a one hundred percent fer-sure fire perfect fit, just like you said!''

AUTHOR'S NOTE

MORE than fifty million adults throughout the U.S. and Canada lack a high school diploma, a number that's growing every day as more and more students drop out of school because of family responsibilities or the need to hold down a full-time job. For these individuals, the doors to further education and job advancement are often barred—drastically reducing their earning potential and severely limiting their chances to prosper throughout life.

If you're one of the millions who don't have a high school diploma, don't put it off any longer. By taking the General Equivalency Development (GED) test, North America's principal high school equivalency exam, you can open doors to new possibilities—including college, greater financial security and a better life for you and those around you.

Call your nearest school board office and tell them you're interested in getting your diploma. Look for the number in the government listings in your telephone book. If you don't find it, call the hotline at 1-800-626-9433, if you're in the U.S., to order an official practice test or find the location of the testing center nearest you. If you live outside North America, call 410-843-6016. Call today—discover who you are and what you really can do.

Many thanks to Stephen Sattler, Center for Adult Learning and Cathy Erwin, General Education Development for the information they provided on adult education and obtaining a GED certificate. I'd also like to thank "Bayou" Bob Popplewell for his fantastic snake info, Denise Stallcup for her insights on the San Antonio

186   THE NINE-DOLLAR DADDY

Fiesta, Diana Estill for sharing her personal experiences and finally, author Eileen Wilks for being a genuine Texan. They all gave freely and generously of their time and expertise. Many, many thanks.

Sultry, sensual and ruthless...

THE AUSTRALIANS

Stories of romance Australian-style, guaranteed to
fulfill that sense of adventure!

This April 1999 look for
Wildcat Wife
by **Lindsay Armstrong**

As an interior designer, Saffron Shaw was the hottest ticket
in Queensland. She could pick and choose her clients, and
thought nothing of turning down a commission from Fraser
Ross. But Fraser wanted much more from the sultry artist
than a new look for his home....

*The Wonder from Down Under: where spirited women win
the hearts of Australia's most independent men!*

Available April 1999
at your favorite retail outlet.

HARLEQUIN®
Makes any time special ™

Look for a new and exciting series from Harlequin!

HARLEQUIN *Duets*™

Two <u>new</u> full-length novels in one book, from some of your favorite authors!

Starting in May, each month we'll be bringing you two new books, each book containing two brand-new stories about the lighter side of love! Double the pleasure, double the romance, for less than the cost of two regular romance titles!

Look for these two new Harlequin Duets™ titles in May 1999:

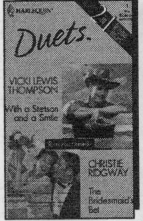

Book 1:
WITH A STETSON AND A SMILE
by Vicki Lewis Thompson
THE BRIDESMAID'S BET
by Christie Ridgway

Book 2:
KIDNAPPED? by Jacqueline Diamond
I GOT YOU, BABE by Bonnie Tucker

2 GREAT STORIES BY 2 GREAT AUTHORS FOR 1 LOW PRICE!

Don't miss it! Available May 1999 at your favorite retail outlet.

HARLEQUIN®
Makes any time special.™

Look us up on-line at: http://www.romance.net   HDGENR

Harlequin Romance®

Coming Next Month

#3547 DADDY AND DAUGHTERS Barbara McMahon
Jared Hunter had just discovered he had not one but *two* adorable two-year-old daughters he'd known nothing about! Cassie Bowles was more than willing to help this bachelor dad with his newfound family. But could she accept his marriage proposal, knowing he only wanted a mother for his daughters?

Daddy Boom: *Who says bachelors and babies don't mix?*

#3548 BEAUTY AND THE BOSS Lucy Gordon
Parted temporarily from those he relied on—his young daughter, Alison, and his beloved guide dog—Craig Locksley was forced to accept Delia's offer of help. So Delia found herself living with an impossibly grumpy but incredibly attractive man. She wanted to love him—if only he'd let her....

Marrying the Boss: *From boardroom...to bride and groom!*

Introducing the second part of Rebecca Winters's wonderful new trilogy:

#3549 UNDERCOVER BACHELOR Rebecca Winters
Gerard Roch had given up on love since the death of his first wife. Going undercover to catch a thief, he never expected to find himself attracted to an eighteen-year-old temptress. But was Whitney Lawrence really what she seemed...?

Love Undercover: *Their mission was marriage!*

#3550 HER OWN PRINCE CHARMING Eva Rutland
Brad Vandercamp is a millionaire English playboy so glamorous that his nickname is Prince! And when Paula meets him at a glittering masked ball, she realizes that she could have found her very own Prince Charming. But they are worlds apart—she's poor, he's rich. Could he really want her for his bride?